'These stories, sassy and stree
poetry, show there is plenty o
Midlands.' *David Lodge*

'An impressive collection of vibrant new voices with a gritty Brummie edge, proof that Britain's Second City is alive, alert and kicking.' *Meera Syal*

'Earnest, vigorous, compelling urban fictions which resituate timeless themes by exploring them in the wrap of our own era. Here we meet father and daughter, brother and sister, women friends, Asian, Black and White, dreamers and runners, in short, a panoply of the young who, materially poor, are rich in passion, in action and in language. English is reinvigorated in these recreations of lives.' *Joan Michelson*

'Surprising, sometimes shocking, often sad, but certainly contemporary. This is unmistakably the voice of youth.' *Mary Cutler*

'The stories are strongly written, and, in their Birmingham settings, have a real sense of place.' *Susan Price*

'In these smart-mouthed stories we hear strong voices surviving the complexity of city experience – and recording it with verve. This is a generation of young writers unfazed by the material world, fascinated by its variety, hooked on the buzz of it all. Here is all the energy of city life in the 90s, and to judge by the quality of writing, yet more signs of great promise for the second city in the decade ahead.' *Alan Mahar*

'Strong, observant stories about urban life for the young as they face uncertain and complicated futures. A sparkling collection from new writers bursting with talent, ideas and energy.' *Alan Beard*

Hard Shoulder

Edited by Jackie Gay and Julia Bell

TINDAL STREET PRESS

First published in 1999 by
Tindal Street Press, 16 Reddings Road,
Moseley, Birmingham B13 8LN

Nick Rendall's 'On the Rails' first appeared in *Raw Edge Magazine*, 5.

Copy-editing: Emma Hargrave
Typesetting: Penny Rendall

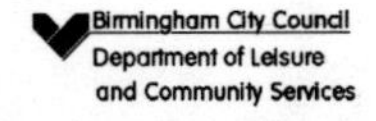

A CIP catalogue reference for this book is
available from the British Library.

ISBN 0 9535895 0 1

Printed and bound in Great Britain by
Biddles Ltd, Woodbridge Park, Guildford.

Contents

Introduction

To outsiders Birmingham is a city populated by a faceless million, a black hole where nothing ever happens, somewhere to pass through on the way to other more interesting cities to the north or south. But Birmingham sucks people in. Like its architecture the city has an uncompromising frankness. As you come in on the A38 from the motorway, the city's skyline sits bluntly on the horizon. *No Bullshit Here,* it might as well say on the signs, the road dipping down and disappearing underneath the city without ceremony.

Historically, people came to the city to make a living, earn their money from the foundries and factories in Bournville, Smethwick, Longbridge, Small Heath, Aston. It was 'the city of a thousand trades', where people made things: jewellery, cars, rivets, guns, motorbikes, taps, chocolate. Sixties architecture and planning brought us the notorious Bull Ring and the carbuncular Central Library. With the collapse of manufacturing industry many of the foundries and the factories that had once made Birmingham great closed. What we have now is a city on the cusp of change. It is reinventing itself: crumbling warehouses have given way to the International Convention Centre, Symphony Hall and the bars, pubs and clubs of Broad Street and Hurst Street.

It may actually be Birmingham's roads which give the city its no-nonsense solidity. The dual carriageways, wide boulevards and undulating ring roads are as much a landmark of the city as the Rotunda, and it was this metaphor that we found strikingly repeated throughout the submissions for *Hard Shoulder.* Birmingham is defined by its roads: the M6 ploughing through, Spaghetti Junction knotted just above the city centre, the radial roads like spokes slicing the city into chunks. People who live here know the city by its roads, bus routes, canals and railways, and we criss-cross these tracks, negotiating our way around the city via towpath and alley, subway and underpass.

When, as editors, we set out to compile an anthology of new writing from Birmingham, we were delighted to find that nearly all the submissions were firmly rooted in the city, because Birmingham's factories, council estates, warehouses and busy streets have rarely been seen as places to inspire literature. The assumption has been that the only interesting things happening in British fiction take place in the capital, that regional writing is necessarily provincial and inconsequential. In addition to such well-known authors as David Lodge, Jim Crace and William Palmer, Tindal Street Fiction Group has begun to redress the balance, producing successful writers such as Alan Beard, Joel Lane, Alan Mahar and Annie Murray. Tindal Street Press intends to take this further, providing England's second city with a first-class publisher.

Judging from the quality of the submissions we received for *Hard Shoulder*, Birmingham now has a growing community of young fiction writers. Here we are introducing a selection that represents something of the flavour of the city. They are all strong stories in their own right, but as a collection they feed into each other, piecing together a picture of a unique and fascinating city and its rarely obvious charms.

What makes the writing fresh and surprising is a sense that here are fictions that try to map the topography of Birmingham: Digbeth, Balsall Heath, Sparkbrook, Handsworth, Selly Oak, Pigeon Park, New Street, Spaghetti Junction. Every one of these writers is interpreting the complexities of the city and adapting dynamically to the culture of rapid change. We see no reason why in future the craft of writing should not be one of the thousand new trades for Birmingham's next century.

Jackie Gay and Julia Bell

B22

Ranjit Khutan

Ashok walked up the hill. It wasn't as steep as he remembered but even so the air caught in his throat. He breathed deeply, inhaling through his nose, holding it for a second and then exhaling. It helped a little. A familiar smell – grass, flowers, ripe tree leaves mixed in with burnt rubber from the local factory – seemed to be moving with him. The smell of his childhood, his park. Only now did he feel he was home.

As he walked upwards, the park spread out below him, but his sight was set on the small flat plateau. He could see the tops of the trees waving, then branches and trunks, then at last the bench – a little more battered than it had been a few years earlier but still there all the same. A litter bin, kindly provided by Birmingham City Council, was its only companion. The gold lettering had partly worn off so it appeared robbed of this, its only jewellery. A tree formed a canopy over the bench, protecting it from wind and rain; claiming it as part of the park.

Perhaps things haven't changed that much, Ashok thought, as he slowly walked toward the bench. Beyond it there were only a few bushes, and then the jagged Birmingham skyline. Mosques, churches, gurdwaras and temples had replaced many of the factories that had previously dominated the view. A tall chimney stack, the only reminder of the city's industrial past, stuck its neck out, bellowing white and fluffy clouds into the almost perfect summer evening sky. He stared at the city, trying to pinpoint landmarks, his arms gripped around his body. He sat down with his eyes still fixed on the horizon. It was surprisingly quiet. The hustle and bustle of the city, only minutes away, didn't seem to be penetrating the broccoli defence of the park.

Ashok jerked his cuff back and checked his watch: 9.00. He threaded his fingers through his hair, fashioning a centre parting, letting his hair fall to just past the tops of his ears. The evening light settled on his skin and a gentle wind brushed his blue checked shirt close to him. He sat upright and pulled his stomach in, patted his hair again, fidgeted about as if trying to find the right pose.

Behind him Baljit ascended the hill. He stopped halfway up and took a note out of his pocket, mouthing the words as he walked: 'Bal. I'm coming home this weekend. Meet me Saturday, B22 at twenty to ten. Hope you can make it. Ash.' As his mouth closed around 'Ash', the figure on the bench came into view and Baljit stopped, his shoulders veering away from the plateau for a second. Then he squared himself, and strode, almost swaggered the last few yards to the bench.

– Ash?

Ashok's head swivelled around and he jumped up.

– Bal. Hi . . . er . . . You got my note then?

– Nah, man, just walking through, said Baljit, turning his palms to the sky. – Course I did, man.

They fumbled a ritual greeting and sat down on the bench, casting glances at each other out of the corners of their eyes.

– We're half an hour early, Ashok said, looking at his watch again.

– Yeah, half an hour. Why did you want me to meet you here at twenty to ten anyway? Bit of a weird time, aye it?

– Oh, er, no reason really, Ashok stuttered. – Forget it. How have you been anyway?

Baljit shrugged, said a few words about his family, enough to satisfy polite requirements. Ashok was staying at his father's, Baljit had been promoted at work. Bitty conversation stumbled into silence.

– It's weird being back, said Ashok, staring at his feet.

Baljit turned to Ashok. – Well, you aye missed much. When did yow get back?

– Couple of days ago, Friday evening. Ashok pulled his eyes away from his feet and looked at Baljit. – It's OK, but it doesn't seem like home. Feels like I'm just a visitor. I miss George Lane.

– Do you miss the factory at the end of the road?

– Is that still there?

– Yes. And the train track at the back of the garden. You sayin' you miss all that?

– I guess I do, Ashok said. His voice was wavering. – I guess I don't know anyone where my dad lives now. Well, I probably don't know anyone round here now, come to think about it, people will have moved on. At least you're still next door to our old place.

They stared at their feet. Ashok's scuffed the ground a little. Baljit's were still.

– Well, I'll swap you any day, Baljit said. – George Lane is just depressing these days. No one's got a job, the houses all falling down.

– At least you've still got the park close, said Ashok, stealing a glance at his friend. – Maybe it's Mom's plastic flowers everywhere that I miss. I know they were tacky and everything but even so . . . His words trailed off down the hill and they fell to silence again.

– Listen to you, you sound like a right whinger, Baljit said.

– Or a whinjit.

– God, I aye heard that for ages.

– Doesn't anyone call you it any more?

– Nah, man, it was only you who used it anyways – tekin' the piss.

– In a nice way though, Ash cut in.

– Yeah, yeah. Course, said Baljit, snatching a glance up. – It's funny the words you use though, aye it? Baljit – Whinjit.

They both laughed, shuffled on the bench, legs flopping out and shoulders back.

– Your accent's changed, said Baljit.

– Only a little.

– Nah, man, you can really tell. I bet yow say graass and paast now?

Ashok stiffened. – I had to, he said. – If you have a northern accent down south everyone thinks you're stupid or something.

– Northern? said Baljit.

– You know what I mean.

– Well, now you're back we'll get yow talkin' like a real Brummie.

– Ar, said Ashok and they both laughed.

– Yow are stayin', aye ya? said Baljit.

The sun slipped a little further down behind the skyline.

– Do you remember the times we used to have here? said Ashok.

– How could I forget? We spent virtually all our summer holidays down here.

Ashok tried to pinpoint when they had first met. They had been neighbours in George Lane since birth, but had only met through their mothers, both excellent seamstresses who worked from home as outworkers. Both their fathers were employed in the factory at the end of the road.

– It was a Friday and we were racing on the back of our

tricycles down the alleyway between our houses. We must have been about five.

– Nah, we must have been seven at least, said Baljit, animated by the memory. – Our dads were going to the social club. It was your idea to spy on them.

– I remember following them down the path, said Ashok. – When they went to the club we just carried on.

– Past the graveyard, said Baljit, pointing it out down the hill behind them.

– Until we came to this place, said Ashok. – Remember, they used to tell us that the bogyman lived here?

– It was quite light but it must 'ave been late 'cos it was summer – a bit like tonight.

– Yeah, it was. Remember those kids playing football?

– I remember eating them plums we took from your dad's tree and spying on them like we were at a footie match. We always used to take something with us to eat when we came here: 'plums, pakoray, parotay', Baljit said, more Asian than Brummie now.

– It was scary, though, especially when that tall one heard us and they chased us right down the hill, said Ashok.

– Yeah, we soon dropped our plums.

The smiles on their faces faded and they shivered, suddenly chilled.

– Even then I knew what 'Paki' meant, did you? Ashok said, a few minutes later.

– I knew it was meant to be bad, said Baljit.

– Yeah, well, you were right there.

– I thought our dads were really gonna tell us off when they found us crying in the alleyway, said Baljit.

– The only reason they didn't was because I got us off the hook.

Baljit laughed and mimicked a childish voice. – What, by

saying, 'W-w-we s-s-saw the b-b-bogyman'?

– It worked, didn't it? Did you ever tell them the truth?

– Nah.

– Me neither. You know what they're like – tell them something like that and they'll go on about all white people being racist and that one day we'll be thrown out of the country.

– Tell me about it.

– I wish I could talk about it to them, though, to try and make sense of it all. I mean look at caste – me being a chamaar and you a jatt – what the fuck does that all mean? It never seemed to matter when we were kids.

Baljit shrugged further down into his Adidas jacket, nodding.

– I keep asking my dad and all he says is, 'It doesn't matter, we are all the same,' but when it suits him he starts comparing caste with others. I remember people at uni asking me about caste and religion – like because I'm Asian I'm some sort of fucking expert. They knew more than I did.

Baljit flashed him a warning look, he knew this tone of voice, but Ashok didn't get the message. – At least we know about the bogyman. There's plenty of things our parents will never talk about, will they? Remember, over there by the tree?

Baljit jerked up. – *I* don't want to talk about it, he said.

– Why not?

– Just forget it, OK, snapped Baljit.

– You're going to have to talk about it sooner or later, Bal. You can't say it didn't fucking happen.

Baljit walked off a few steps, staring away from the bench and Ashok. The whine of a police siren penetrated the park. Other than that there was no noise, but then a sharp ringing startled them both. After a second or two Baljit realized the noise was coming from inside his jacket and he pulled out the offending article, his mobile phone.

– Hello. Oh, hi, Uncle-ji. Baljit walked round to the back of the bench as if to get some privacy in this wide open space. – Yes, I'm fine . . . No, Mom and Dad aren't here . . . I was there. I must 'ave been in the kitchen or sommat. I didn't see you there either but I was in the gurdwara today . . . Where am I now? The interrogation obviously required quick answers. – I'm, er, I'm in the park . . . No, she's at home . . . I'm with a friend . . . Ashok. He used to live next door to us . . . Yeah, the one who went to university . . . Hold on. Baljit turned back towards Ashok, holding the phone away from his mouth. – It's my uncle, he wants to speak to you.

– Which one?

– You know, the one who had that blue car with the yellow doors, hissed Baljit.

– Why did you tell him I was here?

Baljit waved the phone in his face, hushing Ashok, who had no choice but to take it.

– Hello, Uncle . . . Sorry, Uncle-ji. Ashok was about to be interrogated too, and Baljit knew about what. – I know Mom would have wanted me to . . . Just give me five minutes to take a breath . . . OK then, bye. Ashok clicked off the phone and handed it back to Baljit.

– He pisses me right off, said Ashok. – Just like all the rest of them, constantly on about getting married. I mean we're only twenty-two. He looked over at Baljit's back. – We both are, that's one of the reasons why I had to go away. He never used to be so, so, well – you know – like that. I mean, look at his marriage. Now that's one match made in hell.

Baljit turned round slowly and headed back towards the bench. – Some do work though, he said.

– Oh, puleaze. I'd never have an arranged marriage.

– They're not arranged any more; they're introductory marriages now.

– New word, same idea. All pressure and no choice. Anyway, you've changed your tune.

Baljit pulled the note from his pocket and threw it into the bin.

– We had some great times up here, didn't we? Ashok was pacing around, scraping the ground with his shoes as if looking for something. – I wonder what happened to the rest of the gang? Remember that Sukhi? She was a laugh. Yeah, and Mina and Sanj – do you still keep in touch? Well, I guess you do. I wonder if Sukhi still fancies me.

– Well, yeah, said Baljit, hunkering into his coat.

– What, she still fancies me?

– Er, no.

– Well, what then? What's up, Bal?

– Don't get worried, it's good news. You wouldn't know 'cos you aye bin around, innit?

– What is it? said Ashok.

– I can't believe your brother Jas ain't told ya.

– Told me what? said Ashok.

– I'm getting married, said Baljit. – I'm getting married to Sukhi.

Ashok looked around. He walked over to the tree, back to the bench, back to the tree. His face still away from Bal, he said – You and Sukhi are getting married? You're fucking joking, aren't you?

– No, Ash. She was my mom's choice. She's the same age and the same caste.

– Yeah, like it fucking matters.

– She works in a solicitor's office, as a secretary now. She ain't changed much. We've been engaged for a year now. Bit of a shock?

– Well, yeah. A little.

Ashok turned slowly, paced back to the bench with his head down. – Look Bal. Congratulations. I hope everything goes well for you, for you both.

– I know what you're thinking.

– You do?

– I didn't think it would ever happen myself. You can come to the wedding if you like. It's on 22 September.

I might have known, thought Ashok. They're both twenty-two and they first met in B22. Like us.

B22 was the code name Baljit and Ashok had given to the park when they were younger. They came up with it so that their moms and dads would not know where they were meeting. It worked well as there is no B22 postcode in Birmingham. Ashok had introduced Sukhi to Baljit; now she was to wed him.

– B22, said Ashok. – *Our* name for this place. Seems like it worked out quite well for you and Sukhi then.

– We carried on meeting up here after you left.

– So you and Sukhi were, like, together before your mom suggested getting married?

– Well . . . she knew we were friends so she suggested it. An *introductory* marriage, said Baljit, looking Ashok in the face for the first time since Sukhi was mentioned.

Ashok broke eye contact. – So what's happened to Sanj and Mina?

– Sanj is working in computers. Mina got married.

– To anyone we know? Ashok's voice seeped out of the side of his mouth, and he turned his back again.

– Will you tell me what your fucking problem is? Baljit demanded, following Ashok. – You went away to get on with your life. What do you expect the rest of us to do – just sit around and wait till Ash gets back? You're so up yourself, you think the whole world revolves around you. Especially now you got your bloody fancy-pants degree. And in what? Russian! I mean what sort of job is that gonna get you?

Silence. Two figures at the top of the hill, ten feet apart, words falling into the ground between them.

– I'm sorry. It's just that a lot has happened, Ashok said.

– Well, get your head round it. I know it's difficult but it wouldn't have been this way if you had kept in touch.

– I did keep in touch.

– You stopped writing after the first term. Just after your mom passed away. Baljit had moved closer, his eyes steady on his friend.

– I had a lot of work to do, catching up, exams and all that, said Ashok, looking away.

– You saying you couldn't spare a few minutes to call? You may have been over a hundred miles away, Ash, but that shouldn't have stopped you from keeping in touch. When you were at home you had loads of time to come and doss up here and we still got our work done.

Ashok sat back on the bench, looking away. He was quiet. Then he turned to face Baljit. – I know I was being strange. It was partly because of what happened with Mom and all, but there was something else, Bal. I did mention it but you didn't want to discuss it. Just like you don't want to this evening.

– Yeah, well, said Baljit.

– I haven't told anyone. Have you?

– No.

Ashok pulled some gum from his pocket and offered Baljit a piece. Baljit looked up at Ashok and then down to the gum. He reached out and took a piece.

– Thanks.

They both began to fiddle with the little packages to expose the gum. Ashok indicated for Baljit's wrapper. They both chewed; both sat.

– God, it only feels like yesterday, talking about all those things, doesn't it? said Ashok. – I can picture all of the others turning up, late as usual.

– Not early like us, said Baljit, glancing at his watch.

Ashok scanned the park as if looking for the others, but something else caught his eye, something close to him: the bench.

He looked down and then jumped up from where he was sitting.

– Look, look. It's still here, our names are still here! Look: Sukhi, Sanj, Mina, Bal and me. Some fucking tosser's written 'Paki Posse' next to it. He pulled a key out of his pocket and started to scratch away at it. – It's a wonder the council haven't taken this bench away. I guess if they don't empty the bin they're hardly likely to take this away. Ashok was moving round the bench, looking for other marks from their past. – Hey, look, this is still here too, Bal. Do you remember this? Somebody wrote 'IDST' next to it: If Destroyed Still True. Ashok stopped moving. – Is it, Bal?

Baljit flashed him a look, moving only his eyeballs.

– Baljit loves . . . Someone's crossed out the rest.

– Look, I'm sorry I dissed your course, Baljit said.

– What, my fancy-pants degree?

– How was it?

– Fab. Got up when I wanted, stayed out till whenever – and I didn't have the auntie-jis and uncle-jis watching my every move. Oh, the lectures were OK as well.

– Sounds good. I wish I had gone now.

They'd both had plans to study economics in London; that summer, before their A-level results were out. Plans made on this very bench. The results had come through and the plan looked good. But that was before Baljit's dad had been made redundant. With very few skills and no qualifications he found it difficult to find other work. Baljit decided to forgo his place and get a job to support his family.

– Dad still goes on about getting educated. 'It's the most important thing in the world.' Baljit mimicked his dad's voice, overemphasizing the Asian accent. – 'You don't want to work in a factory like me when you're older.'

– Yeah, Bal, but you're not, are you? You've got a good job and you're getting married. I guess that says that life's going well. You were right about my degree, though. The uncles were too. I mean, where's a Russian degree gonna get me?

– Get you a better job than working in a supermarket.

– Hey, not many people land straight into a job at supervisor level.

– Assistant manager now. I got promoted, remember.

– Well done, Bal. I mean it.

– It's the Asian blood in me. Corner shop – supermarket, same thing really, said Baljit, using his hands as if weighing the two options out.

They both laughed.

– Tell me, though. Why did you change from economics to Russian?

– Well, since you weren't studying with me, I thought I'd change and do something else. It sounds good when you tell people and they think it's really complicated. I found it easy.

– Really? Say sommat in Russian then.

For a few seconds Ashok was silent. Something had shifted. The sun was slipping down further and the shadows of their two hunched bodies were lengthening.

– How about you saying something, he said, and I'll translate it.

Baljit looked around him. – OK, say 'What time is it?'

– 'What time is it?' in Russian is – Ashok stopped suddenly, catching the light on Baljit's face. – 'What time is it?' is: *'Ya loobloo tibya.'*

– Ya loblobl –

– No, say it after me. *Ya.*

– Ya.

– Loob-loo.

– Loob –

– Loob-loo.

– Loob-loo.

– Tibya.

– *Tibya*.

– Now, all together: *ya loobloo tibya*.

– *Ya loobloo tibya*. Is that right?

– Yes, perfect.

– Well? said Baljit.

Ashok flushed, just visible in the fading light. – Well what?

– Well, what time is it?

– Oh. Nine-thirty. He shifted on the bench and folded his arms tight round his chest. A chill had settled on the hilltop.

– I don't think I could handle four years of that. It sounds too complicated if you ask me.

– I'll teach you if you like, in your spare time.

– Nah, man. Thanks and all that, but I don't think I'll have much free time what with the wedding and all that.

– Oh yeah, said Ashok. – Forgot about that for a minute.

They sat staring over Birmingham, the setting sun casting perfect soft light over their faces. They made no movements apart from their mouths, chewing.

– It's good to see you again, Ash.

– You too. Didn't think you'd turn up at first.

– Well, here we are.

– Sitting in B22.

– Yep, sitting in B22 and both twenty-two. I wonder if we'll be having another reunion here in another four years – here on this bench.

– Yeah, I wonder, said Baljit.

– The sun's almost set, said Baljit, still looking ahead. – *Ya loobloo tibya*.

Ashok shook his head as if there was water in his ears. – What?

– What time is it? said Baljit, still looking out over the city.

– It's almost twenty to ten but . . . it doesn't really mean that. *Ya loobloo tibya* doesn't mean 'What time is it?' It means –

– I know, said Baljit. – I know.

They both looked straight ahead at the sun setting, followed it down with their heads. Baljit was the first to break off, to turn his head towards the other.

– You wrote it on one of the letters you sent me. And twenty to ten in the note. I didn't have a clue at first.

– I guess you know why now?

– I think I knew all along really, I just wanted to make sure.

– Yeah, it was about the same time that summer evening when we were sitting on this very bench watching the sunset. Remember, we thought we were really grown up. You know – drinking and everything . . .

It had been an August evening, the day they got their A-level results. Sanjay, Mina, Ashok, Baljit and Sukhi had been in the park celebrating. Celebrating on one can of cider. They hadn't needed alcohol that night, but it was a good excuse. They were drunk on the highs of their results. It had begun with the water fight. Mina wanted to sit on the bench and Sanjay wouldn't let her. He was standing his ground; she always wanted her own way. Sukhi was on Mina's side, and for a laugh she began throwing water at him from a bottle she had. They all laughed as Sanjay grabbed her bottle and turned it first on her and then on everyone. There was water and laughter everywhere.

– Mina, your mom's gonna go mad, innit? Sukhi had yelled.

– Quick, said Mina, watch out Suk, Sanj has got –

The girls screamed as water and cider splashed around them. The five ran around B22, carefree.

– Come on, I'm goin', Mom's gonna go crazy, Mina said. She ran off down the path.

– Wait up, we're coming, said Sanjay. He turned to Baljit and Ashok before he ran off. – Yow comin'?

– Nah, man, gonna wait a bit, dry off, Ashok said.

– Me too, said Baljit.

The three disappeared down the hill, leaving Ashok and Baljit on the bench. They were laughing; every time their eyes met they laughed more. Ashok pulled his wet T-shirt away from his body.

– Come on, let's hang them on the tree. They'll dry quicker.

At the tree, Ashok pulled his top off and began to wipe it over his wet chest. Baljit stood staring at him.

– Come here, let me help you, said Ashok. He moved closer. They stared unblinking at each other, then came closer still. They kissed.

The sun had shone on them then just as it was doing now, four years later. Baljit and Ashok finally relived that moment together as they had done so secretly over the past four years.

– I didn't tell anyone. Did you?

– No, said Baljit.

Baljit leaned back on the bench. He looked around and then stretched his arms out above his head, finally resting one on Ashok's shoulders. Ashok flinched slightly but then turned to face him. They kissed just like they had done a few years earlier. From there they could see the whole of Birmingham and now the whole of Birmingham could see them; they didn't care who saw. The emotions and tensions of the evening were finally unlocked, the secret revealed to each other and to B22. As they moved apart they remained facing each other.

– *Ya loobloo tibya,* whispered Ashok.

– I love you too, said Baljit.

Daddy's Girl

Gemma Blackshaw

There's this bloke been hanging around outside. Like a bad smell, Anna says. She's sorted like that. Nothing fazes Anna. Me, I get a bit edgy, 'cos you know, I've got the downstairs front room and everything. It shits me up to see him standing there like he owns the place. And it's not as if he just comes and goes. I mean, he's there, I'd say, constantly. The house, the bus shelter, Vicki Wine, even Blockbuster Video Rental, for fuck's sake. I still maintain that he followed us back from Safeway that time we nicked the shopping trolley. Anna calls it our getaway car. I knew we'd get in it deep for that. What goes around comes around and all that. The trolley's still there out the back with two mattresses we use as sunloungers when the day stretches out long and hot. We haven't been out there as much since Anna burnt her tits. And there's no way I'm gonna sit there on my own. Not with him out the front. Weirdo.

That's why I'm getting the new curtains. I told Dad that the others smelled of fags and curry from the last tenants. That was enough to get him into Ikea and up the motorway. I'm not gonna say anything about the bloke outside. Obviously. Anna says, The pervert just hasn't got a life, that's all. She's probably right. Give it a week and he'll have pissed off. So no, I'm not gonna mention it to Dad. He'd pack me up in the car and take me back. And things are really cool here, 'cept for him out there.

So it's ten o'clock in the morning and I've got the taste of fags in my mouth. I had one out the back before Dad arrived in his big shiny car. I don't think he can smell it but I stand a bit away from him, just in case. I'd never hear the end of it. I finger two stingray ulcers either side of my bite. One week, and I still can't shake them off. I have to move the inside of my cheeks out with my tongue before I clamp my teeth down. And I know he's noticed when he slips me a tenner for vitamin C and Tampax.

I tell him, I'll go down the chemist's straight after you've gone.

He smiles at me. He's nervous here. Two girls in a terrace house.

He says, The drive up wasn't too bad. I did it in just under two hours.

I say, Traffic must've been OK then. It's usually rammed on the M6, isn't it?

Yes, he says, and then silence again.

His face relaxes a bit as he places the curtains on the bed and smooths the material with the flat of his big hand. He never drops things, but positions them. As he steps back he knocks into the bedside table, sending *Marie Claires* cartwheeling to the floor. Dad never does stuff like that. He stammers his way through an apology, and I bend down on the floor to help him pick them up. I can see his back muscles working through his Savile Row shirt. His breath smells of the Extra Extra Strong Mints he keeps in the dashboard of his car. It's close and warm against my bare shoulder. I hope he can't smell the fags on mine. His knees crack as he stands up and helps me put the magazines back on the table next to the perfume he bought me in Duty Free at the start of the summer.

Oh, you like it then? he asks. I wasn't sure, you know, what you'd like.

He smiles at me again, soft and anxious. And I would have told him there and then had Anna not come banging through the front door.

Fucked out of her head. She's just about to say, What a great fucking night, music was banging and oooh girl I looked so hot. But then she sees Dad and slopes off upstairs. She's got blood on the straps of her white plastic platforms. And when she turns out of my room I see two blisters on the backs of her heels. I think about where my needles are 'cos she'll want me to pierce them and drain the shit off. She's crap at stuff like that.

Dad says hello, but she doesn't hear him, leaving him with a half-expectant smile that he clears away with his throat.

He says, Has she only just come in?

And I say, Yeah Dad. She's a bit wild.

And then I look down at the curtains on my bed. Brand new. Run-up, edged, tacked and steam-ironed, white plastic hooks gleaming like shark's teeth on the top hems. We stand on the window-seat I've cleared of nail polish remover and cotton wool. My toes are red and streaky 'cos the polish is too thick. Rimmel or something. The advert said it's chip resistant. We hook the curtains up together.

Dad says he didn't mind driving up today. That curtains were important, especially in the downstairs room. That I should be careful. To watch out for perverts.

He hates saying that word in front of me. Just like he'd never say the word fuck or dick. But I've heard him say stuff like that to other people. Just not me.

I can hear Anna cracking up in the lounge at the mention of a pervert. I could smack her in the mouth when she laughs like that. Dad looks really uncomfortable.

And I say, Oh, it's just something on TV, she's always like that.

I hate it when he's embarrassed. I want to look away until he's together again. We're quiet for a minute, the curtain material catching the stubble on my knees. Twenty hooks each side. Further in until the room gets darker and darker. He lifts me off the window-seat. And I'm laughing. Careful not to scissor my legs over his arms 'cos the hair's sharp and I don't want him to notice. But he touches the long scar on the inside of my leg and says that it's looking better, but he still thinks I should have had stitches in it.

We stand back to look at the drawn curtains. The backs of my knees are sweaty against the bed. Electric blue fabric stops a foot short of the window-ledge.

Bloody hell, Dad whispers.

He always swears under his breath. Just like he always calls fags cigarettes.

Don't worry about it, they're cool, Dad, I say. Curtains are curtains and as curtains go these are gorgeous.

I nearly said fucking gorgeous. You get into the swing of it, swearing. But he's so let down, and he's going on about writing the measurements down wrong and metric conversions and the depth of the window and shit. He's searching through his briefcase and jacket pockets for the piece of paper. I put my hand on the top of his arm and I say, Dad, I like them. You probably can't see much under them anyway, what with the hedge and bins outside. And look, I'm not here much.

He smiles and strokes the hair I washed this morning with Anna's Paul Mitchell stuff down my back. There's a whoop from the lounge and the *Kilroy* music blares out.

I wish you didn't have the downstairs room, he says.

I don't mind, I tell him, and give him a beamer.

Outside the terrace house. Last night's bin bag spills Sainsbury's Economy baked-bean tins out across the pavement. Cats run through the long grass of the front garden. Thank fuck the bloke isn't there yet. I would've said something. I'd have watched Dad walk across the road and punch him in the face. He's strong like that, my dad. I can feel his stomach crunch in and down as he steps on a damp packet of Weetabix the pigeons have been at. As a kid, I'd listen with my ear against his smooth, tight belly for the coffee going down. He told me, There's a factory in there.

Go back inside, love, he says.

He opens the door on a black leather interior with walnut dash. Metallic grey encloses him with a thud that shudders, dull, through my arm. It's an expensive car. He said when he bought it, You can always tell a good motor by the sound of its doors. Jaguars, Porsches, he'd driven them all, but nothing could beat a Merc on the motorway. I look at him through the green-tinted window, at him all kitted up with alarms and mobile phone chargers and Roxy Music CDs. Men like my dad never wear seat belts. He's just about to start up the engine when he opens the car door again and half jogs over to the front step.

Bye, love, he says, and folds my head and shoulders underneath the weight of his arms. He bends his head down to my cheek and rubs silver stubble against it until I laugh. We stand there like that for quite a while. I'm hot in my short skirt when he unravels me and jumps back into the car. He works out every day, my dad. I watch his car slide him away down the street. Anna's in my room.

Sexy bloke, your dad, she says. Don't s'pose you've got a needle and plaster have you babe?

I tell her to fuck off, running upstairs to stick my face under the cold tap and just sit against the cool sides of the bath for a bit.

I'm rubbing the white stripes on my new Nike swoosh trainers with spit when Anna comes in. You've got slug trails on the carpet again, she says.

The window's open. It reeks of evening. Disco music falls out of houses with the front doors wide open, 'cos it's so fucking hot. Pigeons land with scabby feet around a can of spilt Coke, merging, grey and filthy, without footballs and cars to send them exploding into the air. There are enough people in the street, which isn't exactly a main road or a residential area, to make it look deserted. It could be dusk in one of those wild western films with the freak heat of the day and the exotic colours of crisp packets strewn across the pavement like Mexican flowers. The bloke arrived fifty minutes back. He smiled as I looked up. I counted one to sixty through the panic in my chest and pretended I hadn't seen him. That I'm just carrying on AS NORMAL. I decide not to point him out to Anna. She says she's getting bored with the whole bloody thing.

You comin' out tonight babe? she asks.

I've got my silver dress on and glitter across my cheeks. She smiles. That's the girl. Music on full whack. Bass lines and record scratches reverberating around the house. I slip my feet into stilettos with a metal heel, slick vanilla moisturizer up and down my shaved legs.

She says, You smell like ice-cream.

Shall I be mother? she asks. Balancing a CD case on her fat white legs, chopping speed into thin powdered lines.

She's singing, *Aaaah – you've got to give me – got to give me a little – yeah all I want is – all I want is a little – please all I need is* – 'cos it's another Friday between seven and nine.

The Big Night Out. Feet tapping to Pete Tong's Friday night session on Radio 1. Two vodka and Cokes with a twist of orange 'cos we've run out of lemons, sparkle on the side. No ice either. And the trip to the supermarket's another five days away. There's no fucking way I'm going on my own. And Anna says she'll only go when she's good and ready, so we're fucked until Wednesday. I roll up Dad's tenner to snort with. The fizz and sting up my right nostril. Anna's shooting her mouth off.

She says, So there was this bloke, yeah, and he comes up to me and says, 'All right sugar, you're looking beauuutiful tonight,' and I swear he was about FIFTY, so I go, 'Yeah, what's it to you, you old git?' and THEN – get this, yeah – he goes, 'What's a nice girl like you doing in a place like this?' CAN YOU FUCKING BELIEVE IT?!

We shriek with laughter. Chewing gum falls out of our mouths. She lights two fags with her pink plastic lighter with a Spice Girls sticker on the front and hands one over to me.

Anna, I say, it wasn't, you know, that bloke was it? I mean you got a good look and it wasn't him was it?

You're getting paranoid babe, she says. Drop it.

Only, he's outside again, I say.

She pushes me away and stares at him with her best bitch look. When he doesn't budge she sticks her finger up at him and yells, Dirty fucking cunt. I think about pointing out that he wouldn't be able to hear her. But she's steaming tonight, cruising for a bruising, and she'd probably leg it out in her heels to tell him so he heard right. That would really fuck things up.

Leave it, Anna, I say.

But she's up on the window-seat now, shouting through the ventilation slats, Have I got a sodding red light in 'ere or what? Now piss off!

She falls back on the bed and starts to laugh. The honk of a car horn outside and then it's all go for keys fags money lipgloss bankcard, out the door and into a minicab.

Anna yells fuck you out the window as we drive past. I strain my neck round to light a fag away from the blast of the open window, checking that he's not stopping another minicab.

What's he gonna do? she asks me.

Seven sets of traffic lights up the Pershore Road and into the city and I stop reeling through a police description. The no distinguishing facial markings or tattoos routine that Anna's getting fucking bored of hearing, girl. And then we're through the queue at Slag and it's rammed with bodies and the DJ's shit hot. Necking two pills with a shared bottle of Budweiser, sweat shining on our skins like silver. And as we start to dance on the podium, grinning at each other because she's so fucking cool, my mate Anna, I don't think about anything at all.

I'm fucked. Anna, she's been doing it for longer. She knows when the rushes are going to start. When it's time to stick her head down the toilet bowl. She doesn't want to come down and fucks off with a black bloke who's got poppers back at his place. My teeth are grinding, skin tingling, as I call 472 2222 for a minicab. And this bird on the end of the line says there's a half-hour queue. So sod it, I take my stilettos off and tie the straps together for the way back.

Four in the morning. Pissed-up wankers outside the kebab joint sing football songs despite the World Cup being months away. But then it gets quieter and all I can hear are the telephone cables zinging overhead. You get great skies in polluted areas like this. Straight out of sci-fi films. Century Tower splitting all that air. I catch a breeze of car fumes, cruising on past the bed and breakfasts, thick air hitting me like a hot, heavy body. I walk with my head down to watch out for glass and dog shit. Ten minutes through Digbeth, twenty minutes up the Bristol Road, eight minutes till the end of Selly Oak then four up Tiverton Road. I count one to sixty ten, maybe fifteen times until I lose my place and start over again. It's a bit of a routine of mine. Like not stepping on pavement cracks or jumping over manholes. That just makes you look like a tit.

It's never quite dark in cities. The streetlight bulbs have blown towards the end of Digbeth but I can still make out the pavement edge from car headlights that flood the road for a second or two, bringing dustbins and letter boxes suddenly into sight. The cars slow down as they pass me. I can hear their engines pausing before revving right up again. Boy racers. A few of them beep and shout out of the windows. Twats. I can hear a can being kicked on the opposite side of the road. I can see moving shapes but that's about all. I'm so fucked I can make a shadow into whatever I'm thinking about at the time. Anna leaning against the bar with some beer, calling me over until her face gets bigger and bigger and then turns into a crowd of people giving it some on the dance floor. Thinking about it, this is a fucking stupid thing to be doing. I look about for a phone box, thinking that I'll call again and wait under the blue light with the telephone directories inside until the cab arrives. But maybe I should just get to the main road first 'cos I'm not exactly certain about the street names round here. It's difficult to tell one block of flats and public loo from another. I think about the Ready Brek kid with his neon orange outline. That's what I need. I light a fag. I've reached the Lloyds cashpoint, the buttons flashing red and green like traffic lights. The Bristol Road up ahead, a blur of noise and colour like those high-speed pop videos. Got to keep on the PAVEMENT. Got to keep it TOGETHER. I think about Anna doing it with the black geezer on his living-room sofa. Her face red, heart pumping fast from the brown-bottle fumes, like Tipp-Ex only it'll knock your head off. He had a tight T-shirt on, his pecs and biceps moving like the inside of Galaxy Ripples. Anna likes black men. I hear a shout from a lift shaft at the bottom of a block. The lift drops to the floor. And suddenly I think, fuck, what the FUCK am I doing? What about that bloke? My pulse is going like a telephone brrrring brrrring brrrring brrrring. I drop the fag and start to leg it up the street. And I'm saying shit shit shit shit shit over and over again 'cos I'm CONVINCED that bloke's behind me. That he's been there all along.

Streaming past traffic and the Chinese takeaway. Pounding down on the tarmac. On and on and on until I get to Selly Oak, up Tiverton Road number 52 number 78 number 94 and then as I reach the house and make a grab for my keys inside my purse I see that he wasn't behind me after all. He's standing on the opposite side of the road underneath the bus shelter instead. And FUCK, where's Anna when you need her? Shagging some bloke in Balsall Heath. I split across the road to the house. Jam the key in the door. And then I'm in. My feet on the local newspaper and flyers from Mama Mia's pizza delivery.

It shits you up, stuff like this. So you know I'm shaking as I put the double lock on and then CHRIST, the back door and the downstairs windows but then I remember that the landlord nailed the sills down and I'm thinking who can I phone at this time of night but with piss all on the boyfriend side of things I don't exactly have an option here as it's five-thirty in the morning and who the hell would come over anyway with a nutter across the street? Sitting on the floor in the dark underneath my window too scared shitless to run upstairs, to put my music on 'cos the remote control's on my bed and I don't want him to see me. Maybe he thinks I've slipped out the back. Maybe he's in the side alley, back garden, outside loo now. The telephone is just in reach if I slide on my front across the carpet. There's a slug on the floor. A huge glossy bastard sludging all over my cream carpet. They come in through the electric cable hole underneath the window-box, leaving fine silver trails across the floor like that lace pattern dress Dad bought me in Miss

Selfridge last week. Dad. I pick up the receiver.

It rings three times before he answers it. His voice is thick with sleep.

Dad? I say. Dad, I need to talk to you. I'm sorry. I know it's late. I'm, Dad, Dad something awful's happened.

Sweetheart? he asks. Sweetheart, what's wrong, what, what time is it . . . ?

I hear him turn over in bed on to one elbow. The sheets moving as he leans across to the alarm clock with electric digits flashing in his face. I start to cry.

Darling, what is it? It's, it's five-thirty in the morning . . . Darling, God, what's wrong?

I can't get anything out. I'm just heaving into the telephone, kneeling on the floor, carpet burning my skin. He's talking softly, so softly into the phone, rubbing his stubble with the back of his hand.

Darling, please, stop crying, slow down sweetheart, I can't hear what you're saying. You must try to calm down a bit darling, please, I can't hear you. Sshh, love, sshh . . .

I hear the bedside lamp click on and then a fizz as the bulb kicks in. I hear him swing round in bed, sitting up on the edge.

Dad, I say. Dad, there, there's a man – there's a man outside the house. Now. Dad, he's been there for weeks and I don't know what to do.

His voice changes immediately after that sharp intake of breath. Strong now. Calm now. Darling, has he hurt you? He hasn't touched you has he?

No. But he's there outside.

You're not on your own are you? Darling? Where's Anna?

She's out.

I can hear him start to gear up about where the fucking hell is she. Maybe, just this once, I would have heard him swear. But he takes a deep breath.

All right, now have you checked all the doors and windows? He's definitely OUTSIDE, yes? OK, sshh darling, I'm on my way. I'll be there as soon as I can. Turn all the lights on. Go and sit in the lounge. Just let me put some clothes on and then I'll be straight up in the car.

I nod into the phone, snot and tears running down my face. I think of his car, like a streak of silver, clocking ninety-five up the M6. Two hours max, he'd be here.

Come quickly Dad, please, I say.

I click the phone down as Anna walks in with a brown skidmark down the back of her white tight skirt.

I had a bit of an accident, she says, erm, in the taxi actually, still, gets it out of your system don't it?

I laugh so hard I forget about the phone call to Dad. And as she slots a video in the machine and rolls up a spliff for us to share on the sofa, I think, it's cool now. Now that Anna's back. Everything's gonna be just fine.

She unscrews the bottle of Virgin 2000 vodka, handing me the toothbrush mug 'cos we still haven't got round to the washing up towering by the kitchen sink.

Aren't you gonna change? I ask.

No. Fuck that. My head's going too fast. I feel like I'm on the bloody Waltzer. I'll sit on that towel.

Cool.

Anna hands me a packet of Silk Cuts, or Silk Sluts as she likes to call them. Forward planning, she says. I stopped at the twenty-four-hour Shell.

She takes a load of chocolate bars from her denim jacket pocket.

Got these too, she says, they'll take the edge off tomorrow. Don't I think of everything?

I'm slumped on the sofa, my skirt halfway up my arse but I can't be fucked to pull it back down or get a pair of tracksuit bottoms. Anna's still got her sunglasses on her head. They've been there for two days now.

So how did it go with that bloke? I ask.

Shit, she says, couldn't get it up. Takes me all the way out to Balsall Heath and then can't get it up. I mean, can you believe it? I nicked his poppers, climbed out of the bathroom window and got a cab.

She hands the bottle over to me. And then the minutes pound behind my eyelids, forty, fifty, sixty and we're still on the sofa when someone starts hammering down the front door.

I can hear Anna swearing but it's like the sound's down low. Then it gets louder and louder until I open my eyes and see Dad standing in the hallway.

Anna's saying, Erm, we would invite you in, but, erm, it's a bit of a state. She's standing there with her sunglasses on and a shit stain down her skirt hem.

Dad says, Oh, you're back then. God, what's happened to your . . . ? Where's my daughter?

Shit.

I pull my skirt down and inch off the sofa cushion. Dad, I say, Dad I'm sorry about earlier. I, I was really scared. But I shouldn't have got you up here like this. I, I wasn't thinking straight.

His face is unshaven. There's still sleep on the tips of his grey eyelashes. He can't stop blinking, moving from one foot to the other, lifting his hand up to his head again and again.

Where's the man? he asks. The man outside . . . Have the police been here?

Anna says, Erm, excuse me but I need the loo. Nice seeing you again.

He stops with his mouth open and stares at me. For Christ's sake. Sweetheart, what the hell is going on?

I look down at the floor 'cos I don't want to start crying again.

There was a man, I say, outside. But he's gone now. It's all right now.

Dad paces around the lounge, around the Chinese takeout from Wednesday night, the ashtrays nicked from the Beef-eater restaurant down the high street, the bottles of Bacardi and Tia Maria. His hands are on his hips.

He swallows, the tendons from neck to shoulder sticking out like cable wires. He's wearing the white vest he sleeps in.

Right, he says, but it comes up a bit choked and oh fuck, I hope he's not gonna start to cry. Not my dad.

He clears his throat. Right, I think you should come back with me. Come on, let's get your stuff together. I'm not leaving you in a place like this. We can talk about, about this, in the car.

Anna pulls the chain on the loo upstairs.

I don't want to go, Dad, I say.

He's wrapping his manicured fingers around one hand. He's got great hands, my dad.

I'm fine, I say, really. I'm sorry. I just got a bit frightened. And you know, my imagination started going overtime. But, it's fine now, Dad. Honest.

I can't look him in the face.

But, that man, he says, you said, you said he's been there for weeks . . .

I know, I say. I'm sorry.

Look at me, darling? He moves over to where I'm standing and holds my arms down by my side, rubbing my skin underneath his large palms.

I sniff up through my nose and look up at him.

It's OK now Dad. I don't want to go back. Anna's here now. It's fine. I promise. I'm sorry.

He rests his chin on the top of my head, combing his fingers down and down through my hair.

*

Daddy's Girl

I watch him get back into his car. He falls into the seat and lets his head drop back on to the headrest. He sits there like that for two, maybe three minutes, and then rubs his eyes with his hands scrunched up into fists. He leans over to the CD stereo panel and presses play. He doesn't put his seat belt on. Men like my dad never wear seat belts.

A Good Age

Charlie Hill

The Neptune: 5.00

Arch left work that Friday afternoon with a spring in his step, a song in his heart and a big bag of powder in his pocket. It was autumn and a chill breeze blew from somewhere in a clear sky but the sun was doing its bit, sitting and singing in a corner of the high-ceilinged bar.

Arch strolled past St Phil's Cathedral and on towards New Street, a twinkle in his eye. He was twenty-nine years old, a good age to be, the best, young and experienced, quick-witted and sussed. He was also Red Striped-up. With sunshine, the promise of money, pool, more beer and the swagger that can only come with a big bag of powder in your pocket, the boy Archie, Archie boy himself, had this Friday at his feet. He smiled broadly. Town on a Friday often bemused Arch. All those punters wired up with nowhere interesting to go and nothing interesting to do. Today it just amused him. The mess that is humanity poking him, prodding him.

Guwaan, my son. Fill yer boots. We're chock full of comedy joke potential y'know.

Brummie punter after Brummie punter hoved into view and then out again. Look at 'em, lurching along. All life. The hippieshit nonsense merchants and the fat wankers in suits, the apprentice homies, the miserable bastards, the snotty fucks and senile old duffers, the wannabe posh birds, the pie-boys and scrawny sorts, footie shirts and freaks, spoons, spanners, nutters and pissheads, the dickweeds, retards and dreads. By the side of the pavement there were fat Brummie blewters flogging howling burgers. Old people with strange-shaped heads selling newspapers. People begging with dogs. Arch knew them of old from Balsall Heath, his yard. They may not be smackheads now but they were once. Spare us some change please mate, he said to himself when he clocked Punk Sue who dealt and was never short of a bob or two. She was putting on a good show, mind. *EastEnders* theme tune on tin whistle. Pick a key, any key. Bless 'em, every last one. Most of them were lacking in hap or gorm or clue. All of them failed to see the need for such luxuries. Some were smiling. The fat-headed fools. Some were scowling. As he strolled, Arch scowled at the smilers and smiled at the scowlers.

The dialogue kept Arch's feet off the ground and his head in the air. This was what was needed in the centre of town on a Friday. Wherever there were humans there were glorious losers and this was the energy Arch fed off.

From the cathedral it was downhill to his temp agency on New Street. New Street was a hubbub of street art and bad style and as swank as town got. Just being there gave people airs and graces. Arch stopped to pick up his money, flashing his part-time cheque with pride and grinning at those who clocked his jeans. The other temps were all pushing for overtime bonuses with thin-lipped passion. Self-respect? That's a label isn't it? You can get it in Next can't you?

Steady on, steady on. Leave the poor bastards be. It's not their fault. Why should he care?

As Arch left, he looked at himself in the window and whistled tunelessly, 'You satis atis atis fy my soul.' He cashed his cheque and headed away from the big names of New Street towards the coach station down the hill, in Digbeth. From there it was jolly old bifters all the way. The Rotunda marked the end of New Street and the beginning of Arch's city, a steep descent from tourist brochures – such as there were – past Trendy Clothes to tat shops and the Rag Market and crazies and greasy chip papers sweeping like diseased doves on the wing. Down here, the stink of old wet fruit and veg from the outdoor markets balefully hollered in the perpetual gloom. There were always puddles, even today, with the sun out and a perishing breeze blowing through the underpasses. St Martin's church was filthy. The people had no airs and graces. Arch left the smilers smiling and the scowlers scowling. The market on the trawl to Digbeth was a dump. But the walk this way was one of Arch's favourites because Digbeth was boozers, the start of his turf and his Friday night.

On the way down the main drag, Arch clocked a small black lass, fagging it up the hill towards him. She was smart, in that street black sort of way. Recognition was instant as Arch had a good memory for faces, but there had been something else about her he couldn't quite put his finger on . . .

Her name was Louise and he'd worked under her at Samuel's the jewellers on a Christmas job some five years before. She hadn't rated Arch's liberal interpretation of 'morning' and 'afternoon' but he'd liked her.

'Watcha, Lou.' He grinned at her, knowing she'd be flattered that he'd remembered her. Knowing she'd stop for the shortest of spraffs.

'Gosh it's . . . it's . . .' She smiled, her voice like a honey-coated frying pan. That was what he'd remembered of her, that was what she was.

They gave it some chat about old times, the people they'd worked with, shacked up with sprogs or inside for armed robbery. They were both quietly pleased with themselves, Louise because Arch had recognized her and Arch because Louise was pleased. They left each other happy and carried on their way.

Arch had rules about other people and the encounter with Louise was just the job. It was always better to know pieces of people. Sometimes it's the pieces they want you to know. Other times, by chance, it's those they don't. Either way it's so much better than thinking you understand the whole. Who'd want that anyway? Fucking preeverts. Think of the psychic responsibility, maan.

From Louise it was a short stroll to the Neptune at the bottom of Bradford Street. Bradford Street was the start of Arch's stomping ground proper, the industrial heartland of the city's Irish population. It was dirty and dusty and full of fumes and the smell of machine oil and the occasional exotic breath from a halal abattoir.

Now Arch wasn't Irish and he had little affinity with Irish working people. Irish working people did shite jobs for shite money and then backed the wrong nags with the coppers they had left from pissing said shite money up against the wall. It wasn't the shite jobs for shite money that lost Arch. But backing the wrong ponies? Unforgivable.

He also knew Digbeth was as quaint as only asbestosis could be. He'd worked on Bradford Street the once, driving forklift trucks in one of the many battered warehouses of the Victorian factories. The joint made curtain fittings, pelmets and the like. One room smelt of almonds. In there, gnarled old men of forty smoked fags over vats of cyanide gas. Arch had nearly been killed that summer. He lost control of a forklift on a ramp, his life saved by half a girder set in concrete for no apparent reason that had just about stopped the truck from turning over on top of him. On that job, he'd also been given his first pair of steel toecaps. Great times. Despite this, he loved the place. Y'see for Arch, Bradford Street and Digbeth as a whole was the Neptune and the Neptune was Digbeth. The Neptune was Arch's spiritual home. For over ten years, almost since he'd started drinking, he'd worshipped the place.

It was easily the best pub down there; it was probably the best pub in the whole of Birmingham, he'd known a few. He was almost certain that it was the best pub in the entire fucking world. Arch loved pubs. Clubs and chems could come and go but there was always time for a bit of the old knees bend at the Church of Chat. There was no chat with clubs and chems. There was talk about how much you were going to gub and how much you'd gubbed but that was it. The night was all. It was never a part of anything else, unless it was another night.

The Neptune building itself wasn't up to much which was precisely the way any decent boozer should be. Peopled at lunchtime by red old men with a variety of cancers, early evening by yer teaching and real ale set, at night a young crowd, Brum's most unlikely pre-club watering hole. It had a jukebox that switched every night from Grooverider to Dylan to the ubiquitous Yoobies. It had stained glass, leather seats, Victorian tiled toilets, cups of tea, a small pool table and the Guinness, Jesus mother of god, no, better not, the Neptune was run by a family of devout Tims, fuck me then, yeah, lawks a mercy, the Guinness. *The Guinness.* The Guinness was one reason for the Neptune's greatness.

The other was that Arch had been horsing down the stuff for so long in there that he'd become part of the fabric of the pub.

Arch had won pool tournaments in the Neptune in the past. He'd played a league match against a team of twirlies, a working men's club or something, 150 mushrooms and half a microdot to the good. And won. Colourfully. He'd passed out in there. He'd nearly been beaten up in there. He'd sleazed in there, dribbled in there, dealt in there, played chess in there. He'd even had sex in a toilet cubicle, one birthday, with a woman who'd bought him a bottle of champers over the counter. Jesus. Sex in Digbeth is bad enough. But the Neptune bogs? They had stopped seeing each other shortly after that, neither of them sure what they wanted but both of them sure that it did not involve the remotest possibility of any more sex in the shitter of the Neptune.

That Friday, Arch bounced into the pub at around five in the afternoon. He'd decided to shift a bit of his billy in here, have a couple of tots, sort his pool out for the season and then decide what to do with the rest of his night.

'All right Archie,' said Kath from behind the bar.

''Ello Kath,' said Arch. 'Pint of Guinness please. Do you know a geezer called Richard? Captain of the pool team?'

'Rich,' said Kath to one of two boys playing pool, 'this is Arch. He's in the team.'

Richard turned to face Arch. Arch recoiled. Rich looked about twenty-five but he could have been forty. His jaw was as broad as his eyes were narrow. He had a forehead that sank over his face. To say he had been tapped with the ugly stick was to understate the full horror. He'd been in a tragic accident with an articulated lorry-load of your top-of-the-range ugly sticks, all twelve pallets of them. Arch recovered his balance and grinned.

'Richard? I'm Arch. I'm here to pay some money. It's the last day for registering isn't it?'

Richard frowned, a glacial shift.

'Just, mate, just. Should have been yesterday really. I'm

doing you a favour here,' said Richard in a deep, slightly muffled voice.

'Yeah. Cheers mate.' Do you know who you're talking to, you pissant wank rag? You *ugly* pissant wank rag? This is *my* pub.

Arch leant on one side of the bar, Kath on the other, watching the game, sussing the boy out. Now Rich wasn't a bad player but he was one of those sorts who played every shot as though it was his last, tight and tense. He was also a gobshite. And he carried his own chalk, the cardinal sin of any pub pool player.

Kath and Arch were the best two players in the pub. As they watched the gruesome captain of the pool team play mince pool, no words were necessary. The pool was doing the talking for all three of them, and although Arch wanted a rack to kick off his evening, he didn't want to bother with Rich, the poor unfortunate.

'Later then Kath,' he said, eventually.

'Yeah later,' said Kath. 'What you up to?'

'Dunno.' He smiled. Here was where he, casually like, nice and casually like, shifted some powder.

'Coupla beers, you know. Probably stop in at the Eagle, late doors, see how it goes. What about you?'

'Atomic Jam.'

'Oh ar.' Casually: 'Do you need any powder?'

'Nah, cheers. Sorted.'

'Just wondering. See you then.'

'Yeah, later then Arch.'

Mm. Let's see.

It was Friday night.

Arch hadn't shifted any powder.

Arch hadn't had a game of pool.

On the plus side, he was already half minging and headed for Planet Charge. He checked his dollar. He still had, ooh, notes to spare. Although he could have sworn that was a ten spot not a five. Still. Needs must when the devil shits in your briefcase. Balsall Heath beckoned.

The Black Horse: 6.30

Arch strolled out of the Neptune and away up Bradford Street. Behind him, the sun was beginning to set over the Rotunda, the sky raspberry rippled. Sunset over Birmingham. Marvel house. You couldn't get that anywhere else. Absofuckinglutely unique.

Arch burst into song. 'It's all too beeyutiferuhul, it's all too beeyutiferuhul . . .' and it was. Aside from the fact that he had to play in the same side as Rich next week, everything but everything was right with the world. Beer.

He fingered the bag in his pocket.

Drugs.

Money.

It was then that Arch suddenly thought of emptying his sacks.

Maybe this was due to Kath. He'd never really fancied her, but somehow, women being efficient, behind a counter . . . Whether it was women in authority or subservient women there was something about them. How many barmaids had he fucked? Why did he always fuck barmaids?

To Arch in his jollier moments, when he cared, that was all people were. Who they fuck and don't fuck and how they fuck 'em and why they don't.

Arch knew he was lucky when it came to sex. He was a good-looking, charming sort who had fucked a lot and sex always breeds sex. If he wanted a fuck he was usually able to get one. That was as far as it went, though. Arch liked to keep sex as sex.

Let's face it. There's sex and relationships.

Relationships were always hot summers. And who

wanted clammy hands on the back of your neck when the sun was evaporating milk and melting the gum on the pavement?

No ta.

On a practical level, if you were in a relationship you missed out. You could no longer, by definition, enjoy the unrivalled gleeful sacrament of pissing in the sink. Then there was the sex itself. What was it Lees said? Three hundred fucks and that's your lot. After that the relationship was over.

And I mean dead.

Arch had given it a go, mind. He'd lived with women three times, well, six if you counted the lass he was not too sure about. Any road up, Lees was right. It was always the same.

'Darling, shall we indulge in a spot of role-playing sex tonight?'

'Ooh darling, that would be fun.'

'OK schnookums. I'll be Father and you can be Mother.'

Jolly old fucking bifters.

That Friday, Arch was having non-relationships with two women. The choice between them was his one decision of the night. On the one hand was his regular non-girlfriend or co-fuckee, Rachel, with whom he was having the most intense, strung-out, no-strings non-relationship in the history of innovative human disasters. They were both free to sleep with anyone they wanted but how this was possible, when they were sleeping with each other all the time, was tricky.

Arch hadn't seen Rachel for, oh, two days now and so on Bradford Street, with his testicles full of Guinness and his loins loosened by alcohol and the thought of sex gambolling through his cold yet sunny head, she was right up there, in with a chance. But it was a slim one. Tonight Arch deserved the best. And tonight, Arch knew that Lees was in town.

Lees was an amazing woman. If Rachel was a camping trip where you didn't leave the tent 'cos you were too busy making shadows, then Lees was fucking on a bouncy castle at the edge of the world.

Lees was five years older than him, a single mother and a robust, womanly woman, with sags in all the right places. She exuded an upfront sexuality of elemental power and a self-sufficiency in everything but the Department of Cock. To this end Arch would often announce himself as the Man from the Ministry.

He had fancied Lees from the moment that he'd turned to her in a pub and introduced himself with the words, 'Can I come back to yours?' and she'd said, 'Yeah.'

She was seeing someone at the time, but he was away on hols with their three babbies. Lees had said, 'Well, no one's faithful are they?' and Arch had seen no reason to disagree and they'd abused each other, randomly, ever since. Yeah, tonight Lees was going to get lucky.

Arch arrived at the Black Horse for a rack of pool and surveyed the bar. The pub was full of workers, short punters who looked at Arch's long hair with undisguised distaste. Now Arch had done a lot of work in his time, office stuff, even civil servanting for a suspended stretch, but he was as proud of his patented six-months-on-six-months-off regime as he was of any of his career achievements. Few of his jobs had lasted beyond the first rays of summer and few of his spells of staring aimlessly at the funny boards down the dole had seen him tiring of white cider and lines of whizz.

Arch stood at the bar and made a show of looking at his payslip. Just to let them know, like. He would play a rack or two, just to put himself in the mood and then he'd sort himself a woman. He played. He won. He was happy. He rang Lees.

'Lees. Me old fruit. Have to be quick. In a call box. How's it going?'

'Good, good. I'm coming over to Brum later. There's an Atomic Jam on at the Que Club. You coming?'

'Er nah. Don't think so. Bit potless.'

'Oh yeah? Where are you now?'

'The Black Horse.'

'Getting pissed?'

'Having a couple . . .'

'Getting pissed.'

'Nah, nah. Well maybe. What are you doing after? I'm on to Satan's mebbe.'

'Dunno.'

'Well dive on over if you fancy it late doors. If I'm not up, bang hard.'

'I'm thinking of letting Pete come out tonight so I don't know. He's been wanting to come to Brum for ages and I haven't let him. If I don't see you later, I'll give you a ring, yeah?'

'Yeah. Have a good one Lees. Don't overdo it.'

'See you Arch.'

Arch sometimes suspected that Lees was not a big fan of his boozing. He suspected that most of his friends and acquaintances thought that on the quiet. With most of them he didn't care. Lees was different. She was a *friend*, a friend who he had sex with. He'd never said anything about her little habits, mind. She was up to around six pills a night these days, having caned the little bastards summat rotten. And Christ knows how much powder. And the skunkers. Arch had smoked too much of that, only needed a puff to give him the fear. No one could tell Arch that any of this was any better for you than drinking. He knew. He'd been there. Banging as much of everything as anyone he knew. Snorting crushed Es. Being up for three days. Fucking with his head. The trouble with chems is knowing when to stop before you lose it. With alcohol you don't have that problem. You stop when you pass out.

Oh well. Plan B. Best shout Rach.

Arch knew straight away that something was wrong, as you do.

'There's something I've got to tell you,' she said.

'Is it you and Dick?'

'Yeah.'

'But you live with him. Have you had enough of me and you?'

'No. I don't want it to end.'

'You should have thought about that. Living with someone is tricky, y'know? Still, I suppose we said it was OK. When did it happen?'

'The night before last . . .'

'So why didn't you tell me last night?'

'. . . and last night.'

'Rach, that's not on. That's bang out of order. We said we'd be honest.'

'I know. I'm sorry.'

'Anyway, you said that everything was going great.'

'It was. It was just one of those things that had to be done. I don't want to see him. He's *Dick* for God's sake.'

Arch hung up. On this night of all nights, when he had money, beer and drugs, he should not be denied sex. It just wasn't on. He ordered a cheap double whisky, his annoyance intensifying with the hit of the scotch.

What a fucking idiot. What the fuck is she doing? What does she want? She lives with him for fuck's sake. I mean we're both slappers yeah, that's the whole fucking point of it. But slags have standards too. Heh heh. That's good, that. Slags have standards. No, it's not standards, it's common fucking sense. You don't shit on your own doorstep. What the fuck was she up to? That fuckin' Dick an' all. What a wanker. You don't shag your mate's girlfriend. Or non-girlfriend. Course you don't. *Chum*. *Geeeez*. Fucking wanker. I dunno. I mean. What the fuck do you do? What a fucking performance.

Arch phoned Lees.

'What the fuck,' he said. 'You know I told you that lass I wasn't seeing told me she was loving every minute of it, well she's only gone and fucked her housemate. Twice. Without telling me. That was the whole point, that we were honest with each other. I know him as well. He's a mate. What a wanker. I dunno.'

'I thought you said it was an open relationship?'

'It was. I mean I shagged my ex. But only once. And I told her straight away. We said we'd be honest with each other.'

'You're jealous.'

'No. No actually I'm not. I wasn't into her at all. But I told you, the sex was fucking brilliant. And, and, you don't shit on your own doorstep do you?'

'No you don't. But I told you didn't I? How often were you seeing her?'

'Three or four times a week. Maybe five.'

'Maybe five. Well that's not casual then is it Arch? Casual is once a fortnight at the most. More than that it's not casual. And if it's not casual you can't see other people and be honest about it, you've got to lie. You remember that morning we were in bed together and Phil came round and was banging on the door for an hour because me car was outside and he knows I never go anywhere without me car and he thought I had someone in there? He's still convinced I did. He keeps asking me. I just lie. You've got to.'

'Yeah. You're right, Lees.'

''Sides, fuck her, she was a dull bastard. I never liked her.'

'But the sex . . .'

'I know. But what you've got to do now is get her back somehow. It's a karma thing isn't it? If you've been yinned by someone, you're gonna want to yang 'em good and proper aren't you?'

Arch pissed himself chortling and snorted whisky snorts.

'Anyway Arch, have a good night, I've got to go.'

'Yeah. Cheers Lees.'

Arch hung up. Gawd bless Lees and her indefatigable skill at turning poisonous bile into toxic phlegm. She really was a comfort, a treasure. If you were who you fucked Arch was suddenly glad to still be fucking womanly, sensible, bitter, twisted Lees and not the insipid, scrawny, simple-witted Rachel. What had she given him apart from six months of great sex? What did she have to offer except, well, those impossibly long and sensuous fingers, sweet, peach-sized breasts, muscles that could squeeze the juice out of a banana, and the way she gently, oh so gently . . .

Whoa. Hang on a minute there Arch me old son. You're not doing yourself any favours here y'know. Besides, why do you need sex tonight? Sex is for when you don't have the money for beer. Tonight you've got Guinness to drink and pool to play. Pool. Yeah. Think pool.

Think pool.

Arch liked pool. There were times when Arch was playing pool and there was no prospect of any sex, that he used to think that pool was better than sex. It was a language all of its own. You could walk into any dog-rough shithole in the country and if there's a pool table and you speak the language, you're all right. There were times when Arch had been out and about and he'd conquered places. Just taken them over and left them a hero. No blood spilt nor anything like that. Just the sheer overwhelming superiority of his command of the language.

The trouble was, by now the Black Horse was beginning

to fill up with people who didn't know shit from pudding. Right now, Balsall Heath and the chancers of the ghetto were beckoning more enticingly than ever. He played a final couple of smoky racks on the Black Horse's poxy table with poxy punters who thought that his hair meant that he was a chuffer, drank a couple more swift Guinnesses, then counted his notes.

Shit, hang on a minute, I'm sure I had more than that. Oh no, not that old twenty into tenner gag again, you're not impressing anyone, I know exactly how it's done. Ho hum.

Arch left the Black Horse feeling slightly pissed. He felt slightly hungry and slightly noised up and wondered how long it would be before the place stopped reminding him of Rachel.

The Albert: 8.00

On the bus the kid sauntered unconvincingly up the stairs. It smelt of piss and weed. At the back were two young puffas giving it some chat and smoking skunk.

'He don't know you know, I'm telling you. You don't *do* dem kinda ting.'

They give Arch the eye. Arch knew they'd be expecting him to sit down the front but they were only picknees, trying the part for size, and he'd had enough beer to face them down. He sat big in a seat two in front of them and sparked up a fag. This is the way to Balsall Heath, boys, my yard. Fuck it, I'm carrying drugs. Nice powder. Anyone carrying what I'm carrying knows something or someone. So don't. OK? Just don't.

The bus slid through the razor-wired infant schools and tower blocks of Highgate and Arch chuckled so the boys could see he didn't care. He imagined them menacing the back of his head. This was all part of the game. Any trip to Balsall Heath, any feelings about the place, came down to violence and how you coped. Many people wouldn't live there and Arch knew that the kids who did liked to call it the ghetto. But Arch had never been mugged. He'd never been threatened with a shooter. He suspected that this was because he knew too much. From experience Arch knew there were two types of dodgy punter in the ghetto, the don and the weasel.

The dons were your top dogs.

Your don swaggered. Your don only dealt with other dons.

The weasels were your snideboys. The lowlife. Weasels wanted to deal with dons.

Of the two, the weasels were the most dangerous. Provided you'd let it be known that you understood the food chain, you could always walk away from dons. You could not do that with weasels. Sometimes you just had to face them down, show them you knew the score. Leave them thinking you know something or someone they don't. Cardinal rule. No matter how big or hard you are, there is *always* someone somewhere bigger or harder than you.

All of this caper was second nature to Arch now. He would never completely relax and would never want to but Balsall Heath was more than other people being afraid of violence.

Balsall Heath was encounters.

Balsall Heath was about seeing a man leave his house at five in the morning to visit his neighbour and be followed respectfully by two sheep in single file. It was about approaching a group of five lasses in the middle of the road practising a cappella vocals and dance routines around a knackered transistor radio and not being sure if you were going to be hit over the head with a half house-brick or a close-harmony rendition of 'We Are Family'. It was about Indian homeboys saying, 'You shouldn't do that you know what I mean. We're just friends having a friendly game of cards. I've got this cousin right . . .'

It was about Asian old boys and girls lounging in their front gardens full of spinach and watching the world go by. It was about the flaming neon karehis of the balti houses that flash and clash down the Ladypool Road like Vegas come to Birmingham. And the rave newsagent run by a family of street Sikhs that stays open until ten with the BIG lover's rock party starting at eight. And the house that has a sign in its window that says 'Ame Run Tings'. And the shops with fruit and veg the colour of saris and spice sections that sing with a siren scent. And the tunes. And the rats. And the weasels. And the rats.

Arch was under no illusions about Balsall Heath. It was not a place for voyeurs or dreamers or those who imagined they could keep their head in the stars while they gazed at the gutter. He knew there were times when it could get on top. But it was just all so much more *satisfying* than anywhere else.

On the bus, Arch made sure the bad boys could tell what he was doing and took a dab from his bag of quality powder, his ghetto ID. Later *boys*. I'm hustling, *boys*. With connections.

The two of them got off the bus the stop before Arch. They hadn't said anything the whole time he'd been on there. As they walked past him they chortled and Arch suddenly felt a prick. He needed the pub, the security of a pool table. He got off the bus and walked past Zaff's all-night kebab and homeboy joint, two drags on a fag and he was at the Albert, a genuine shithole up a ghetto side street, the best place to come if you were needing a break from dribbling over potential co-fuckees. In here it was the old women that did the dribbling. The only youngsters in there would be sex offenders if they could be bothered. The jukebox gave you twenty-seven credits for a quid. The only reason for the pub was the table. This was nice, sweet as, the best in the ghetto.

Arch was looking to get his third or fourth wind of the night and could think of no better way to go about this than to get on a roll on the Albert's table. After ten minutes of grafting, playing every shot as though it was his last, tight and tense, Arch lost a rack to a professional bookies' pal who had thumbs instead of fingers.

Arch christened him Paddy O'Digits and smiled to himself but it wasn't enough.

Arch was glum.

By now the whizz had kicked in and had dulled the raging heat of the alcohol in his head. He needed some energy to feed off other than his own glorious human losses. Then he remembered Chris. Yeah, why hadn't he thought of it before? Chris, his one regular mucker, the one geezer he could talk pissed-up nonsense to without fear of being made to feel as though he was talking pissed-up nonsense, his mate, his oppo. There he'd been getting shambolic and feeling mis and he'd forgotten who his friends were.

'All right geez,' said Arch.

'Archie. Geez. How are you?'

'I'm pissed.'

'Yeah?'

'Yeah. Me doris. Or rather me non-doris . . .'

'Rachel?'

'Yeah. Tuppenny hooer-bag. Only gone and kicked me into touch.'

'But I thought you weren't seeing each other,' said Chris.

'Well yeah, but we weren't seeing each other four or five times a week. She shagged that Dick geezer she lives with, didn't she?'

'I thought he was a mate of yours?'

'Well yeah, sort of. So,' said Arch, 'you coming out? Have a few beers? Check out the chickolitas?'

'Not tonight Arch. I'm off to Worcester to see Sarah.'

'Didn't you go there last weekend?'

'Yeah. And I've got some news of my own. You know I said we were looking for a place together –'

'Vaguely,' said Arch.

'Well, we've found somewhere.'

Arch's night had taken another turn for the worse. Everything, in fact, had gone to cock.

Chris. Geez. What are you saying?

OK. So it had been on the cards. But.

Chris was leaving Balsall Heath. Leaving the ghetto. So what was going on? Arch had never felt superior to punters who'd changed their life for a lifestyle, gotten mortgages and pensions and fucking babbies. This was fucked up, sure, but Arch knew that everyone was fucked up. He was because he wanted more than this. But he'd always been happy that he was giving it a go, that he saw more than the office clock during the course of a day, that he saw the next drink drug fuck tune in glorious Technicolor every waking hour.

Now, suddenly, pissed up in the Albert, Arch was not so sure. Maybe these punters saw everything an' all. Maybe, in the end, you just had to accept that there was nothing you could do about being fucked up one way or the other so you may as well be fucked up and at peace.

Suddenly Arch's anger turned to fear. He had no desire to become a freak, the last of a breed. He was petrified that he was destined to be warmed up at shite dinner parties like so many crusty fondue dips.

Arch was minging drunk.

The Eagle: 10.00

The kid walked through the crusties in the bar, into the small, smoke-filled back room and up to the pool table. The room was full, puffas with gold, old-timers, short hairs and ghetto women. The jukebox was playing a fucked-up mix of 'Mr

Lover Man'. The kid took a swig from his bottle of Newky Brown, looked around him at the dreads and the dealers and took some small change from his pocket, which he examined, carefully, rearranging the coins into their order of size. He stared at them in his palm and then looked at the two markers sitting on the side of the table.

He casually dropped a penny down into line and stood, his elbows resting on the narrow wooden shelf that ran along one wall.

Two young weasels stared at him, wondering what this hippie was wanting. The boys smoking reefer and drinking barley wine in the two corners of the room furthest from him, the dons, had also clocked him and looked at him with interest. All of the dons recognized him. He was a regular in the back pool room of this ghetto pub. Most of them knew him to greet. Some of them had even shot a rack or two with him in the past. Tonight though, something was different. His jeans and denim jacket had obviously seen better days and his T-shirt hadn't been washed recently, but that wasn't it. The kid was a good-looking boy but he was in a bad way. He looked weary of the world and under his eyes were grey bags. His eyes looked tired and sore and he blinked often in the smoke. It looked like cash worries. Or woman worries. Or maybe just too much beer.

Mutton

Alison Waller

'Look at the meat. Really look at it. And smell it. It should smell fresh and sweet. There's nothing nicer than the smell of a really fresh shoulder of lamb. Of course, we're here to learn how to enrich it – rosemary, perhaps; thyme, lemon juice – developing all the flavours and aromas. But you really must concentrate on the meat itself first.'

Heather gazed at the fatty slab in front of her. It was pale pink and oozing watery blood. She glanced around her and then sniffed deeply, close to the meat, enjoying the smell and feeling her toes tingle. She almost forgot the other cookery students. They muttered to each other and prodded their ingredients unenthusiastically. There were a couple of old wispy women in paisley, several severe forty-somethings with brisk haircuts, a rather anaemic-looking man wearing faded jeans and a checked sweatshirt. This particular man was looking at Elaine, the energetic tutor, with great interest. He looked down at the lamb, back to the front of the room and down once more. He smiled, then frowned, clearly puzzled but desperate to understand.

Heather understood Elaine. She didn't understand the frizzed blond hair or the cropped top, and cookery jargon passed her by, but she knew the joy of the smell of fresh meat.

Two months earlier, she had been sitting drinking coffee in the staff room with Charlotte, a younger, dark beauty and already Heather's superior. Another colleague, Jeff, lurked in the background reading his paper but listening too, nodding and grinning. Charlotte was staring through biscuit-coloured blinds at the concrete and cars of Spaghetti Junction in the distance. A warm brown haze tinted the air.

'God, this place gets me down.'

Heather smiled politely.

'What about you, Heather? I mean, this place seems to be your whole life. What did you get up to last night?'

'Um, I don't really do much. I'm usually so tired after all the overtime . . .'

'God!' Charlotte hissed out her breath. 'I couldn't cope with just this place. I need something else.'

'Yeah,' said Jeff, shaking his sports pages sympathetically. 'You need to meet people outside work, you know? Did I tell you about Karl? I met him last night at the Nightingale and I really reckon it could work.'

'True love again then, Jeff.' Charlotte yawned. 'But he's right about getting out and about, Heather. You have to have more to your existence, find out what turns you on and go for it. Make the most of life.' She knocked back the coffee and dashed to her desk.

Heather was left, in her calf-length skirt and floral blouse, to consider. She disliked the way Charlotte spoke – always sounding as though her mind was on sex. But still, something in her was stirred and shaken out. What did turn her on?

*

'I don't want you to be ashamed about touching the meat.' Elaine was bounding around her display bench more like an aerobics instructor than a cookery teacher. She was glaring at the women to urge them on, and smiling at the men to show how much fun marinating lamb could be. All the time she was pummelling and slapping the chunk of meat, extolling the virtues of firmness and sweetness and the right amount of fat.

When the class finished, Heather stumbled out of Bournville College into a muggy evening. She couldn't stop shaking; her whole body felt electric, her mouth was wet, her head light. She wasn't thinking in words or pictures but in smells and textures. When the pallid man in jeans approached her she hardly noticed him and seemed to be ignoring him until he patted her upper arm. She twitched, shivered, then managed to smile nervously. The man – Glen – didn't seem to notice her sweaty skin and her flushed nose. He just smiled back.

'Are you a beginner?' He looked earnest and very interested.

'I like . . .' She hesitated, searching for a way to say it. 'I like . . . food.'

Glen smiled again. 'Me too. And drink. Would you like one?'

'What?'

'A drink, shall we go for a drink?'

'I don't know why I ever thought Karl and I had something going. We're too different, you know? But hey, Charlotte, there were these twins in there last night. Michael and Chris. They were amazing, I mean, just textbook looks. And I think they both fancied me. What am I going to do? I mean, they're both gorgeous. It's not that I want both of them – I'm not into weird stuff like that – what d'you think?'

Charlotte muttered 'bollocks' into her coffee and reached out for the radio switch. Heather's station – melancholy violins, perhaps Mendelssohn – quickly decomposed, readjusted to Radio 1.

'This song's great, innit?'

'It's teeny-bopper fodder, Jeff.' Charlotte tapped her foot anyway. A young, unusual beat. 'Hey, Heather, wasn't it your big night out yesterday? So what can you cook now?'

Heather was sitting at the table, a reddish tinge to her face, embarrassed. 'Well, last night we cooked lamb with rosemary and a herb sauce. It was quite basic, introductory, you know.'

Charlotte unwrapped her sun-dried tomato pasta salad. 'Is it all going to be meat?' she said. 'I don't know how you can do that. I know we're not all veggies, but how can you stand to even touch meat, raw meat? Ugh.'

Heather tried to smile. 'Well, you know, it's not so bad. I . . . The touch of the flesh is not so bad.'

'It depends on what flesh you're touching,' said Jeff, emerging from behind the Birmingham *Evening Mail*. 'You need a man, not cookery classes, Heather. I know, you have one of the twins, I'll have the other.'

'Jeff!' Charlotte stared out her disgust, but caught hold of the words and twisted them. 'Were there any men there, Heather?'

Heather was eating her ham sandwiches unhappily. She desperately wanted to run away; she felt exposed and ashamed.

'Yes,' she said suddenly and loudly, 'yes, there were men there. I even went for a drink with one. Glen. We might even meet again after class next week. He's very nice.'

'Blinding!' said Charlotte, grinning. Heather turned back to her lunch.

Heather and Glen sat in a lively pub, crushed into a corner table with their half a lager 'n' lime and pint of bitter.

'Can I tell you something, Heather?'

She nodded and a stray piece of hair fell across her forehead.

Glen smiled gently. 'You're letting your hair down. I've been watching you for the last few weeks, in lessons. You really get into the cooking, don't you? It's amazing watching you. You seem to put everything into it, everything into preparing the best meat possible. Passion. Did you know you had passion? *I* know.'

Heather's half-pint glass froze at her mouth. A dribble slipped down her chin and fell on to her blouse, on to its tiny rosebud pattern. She blinked and put her drink down, cringing. The cookery classes came back to her in a rush of fleshy, juicy, bloody pictures with Elaine's chattering filtered through like mindless background muzak. The sensual tearing of pure chicken breast, the soft squares of braising steak, like cool, damp fingers, the smell of cut, almost living meat.

Heather found herself staring, mouth unattractively askew, bladder aching, chest blazing. Glen's laughter jolted her back into real terror and shame, and her bladder shifted a little. 'Excuse me, I need to . . . I have to visit the Ladies.'

When she returned, reddened but neat and calm, Glen had bought fresh drinks. He held out his hand, she gazed at it.

'I'm sorry, Heather. It was out of place for me to talk so blatantly, so outspoken. I do believe you are a very passionate woman, but I really didn't mean to suggest anything inappropriate.'

She smiled and nodded and drank.

'But now the subject has come up –' he paused and scratched at his patterned jumper '– I think perhaps we should try and further our friendship a bit.'

Glen's flat was dark, bachelor. He fussed around, putting on wall lamps and music and fumbling for glasses. He led

Heather to the kitchen and proudly opened the upright fridge. Two gleaming steaks, almost maroon in colour, lay outstretched on a pale yellow plate.

He said, 'I'll cook them for us. You remember the first . . . no, it was the second class, wasn't it? Elaine showed us how to cook the perfect steak; medium rare, succulent. What did she say? "You *must* choose the best possible cut, then really really really look at the flesh and touch it!"' Glen sniffed in amusement, 'She's a funny lady, that Elaine.'

'Pretty too.'

'Pretty? Yes I suppose. Well, no, I'd say not. She's not half as classy as you, Heather.'

Heather looked at the floor, avoiding the glare of the sirloins. 'Did you say you had a rat?' she said suddenly.

'Rupert? I'd forgotten I'd told you about him. Come and see, he's in the bedroom.'

The bedroom was decorated in black and grey and white. It was also heavily mirrored and low-lit, giving a sense of shadow. In the corner was a large, split-level cage with a draped black cloth over the top. Heather tiptoed over and crouched down. In the bottom of the cage was Rupert, a lean white rat with clear pink ears and tongue. He was chewing at cucumber and lettuce and seeds and what appeared to be red meat.

'Rupert likes steak too. I hope you don't mind him taking a share.'

Heather giggled. 'Not at all, I think it's funny.' And she did seem to find everything funny at that moment, or at least amusing. She had drunk several lager and limes at the pub, and already two glasses of wine out of Glen's cheap decanter. The unease she had felt when Glen suggested a bite to eat at his flat seemed ridiculous. Her worries about his urgent manner and the way his careful distance swerved into overpowering intimacy were slipping away. His compliments flattered her and his rat was charming and his flat was exciting. Heather could feel her good sense oozing away, but it felt natural and did not seem to matter. She was sure she'd feel more with it after a steak dinner.

Rupert finished his bloody meal and Heather eased up off her knees. She found that Glen had closed the bedroom door, shutting out the gentle glow of the lounge lamps, leaving just a gloomy tinge of light. Just enough to illuminate Glen drinking steadily out of an almost full whisky glass. Heather giggled again, then snorted and tripped over something hidden in the darkness, falling slightly so that she leant half on the bed.

Glen smiled and moved to help her up. His hand was unusually sweaty and, normally so courteous, he crushed her fingers, breathed heavily into her face.

They sat together on the black quilted bed and held hands. Heather was trembling. She felt terrified but light-headed and daring. When Glen began to kiss her hand she was completely stunned, frozen in incomprehension. His kisses travelled up and down her arm, touching the rosy edges of her sleeves. They were solid kisses, determined, almost workmanlike. When he reached her mouth he didn't look into her eyes, but resolutely tasted and pecked and swallowed in air. Heather closed her eyes and didn't worry as much as she would have thought.

Glen began to undress her hurriedly. Before, if Heather had ever imagined this moment, she had pictured herself sensuously stripped in subtle darkness, down to matching bra and knickers, left looking like a model in an ice-cream ad. But Glen undid her blouse and threw it on the floor, then he struggled with her bra and released her breasts as quickly as possible. Even in her muddled, drunken state Heather sensed the ugliness of this and felt frumpy and misshapen. Her skirt bubbled around her stomach and her breasts tugged downwards. She wriggled away violently, catching Glen on the chin. He fell backwards.

'Oh, I'm sorry,' said Heather.

'No, I'm sorry.'

'I hit you . . . did I hit you badly? I mean, are you hurt?'

'No no. But Heather, am I going too fast? I don't mean to . . .'

She looked at him. His hand was trembling and he was hunched up slightly, looking uncomfortable. She felt uncomfortable too, slightly sick and cold and ugly. But something kicked in her mind. She couldn't work it out but it pushed her onwards.

'Perhaps you find it difficult to start with someone new.' Glen sounded desperate, clutching out at her. 'Look, whatever you want to do, we'll do it. I just want to make you happy.' He reached her shoulder and touched it, grasping further. 'I'll do whatever you want. Whatever turns you on.'

The words electrified Heather's mind. They were like a blue neon light, making everything seem clear. The wine swirled in her head and around her body and she suddenly knew what she wanted. She wanted to be dangerous; she wanted to be turned on. And she knew how to do it.

'Wait here,' she said and, leaving Glen half sprawled on the bed, she headed for the fridge.

'Hey, Heather, you look rough. Out on the town with your man last night, were you?'

'Well she can't be as shagged out as me. Chris is so energetic. I sometimes wish I was that young again.'

'God, Jeff, it's the same from you every day. Heather, tell me all your juicy details. I haven't had a good bit of gossip for ages.'

Heather lingered on the word 'juicy'. It sounded nice, it sounded fun, it sounded opulent. She gazed down at her cup of tea and smiled faintly. It sounded nice to her anyway.

'Heather?'

'What? Oh, I had an early night last night.'

'I thought it was your cookery lesson and sesh down the pub with Mr Right.'

'Well, it was the last one; we said our goodbyes.'

Jeff nodded knowingly and Charlotte frowned. 'I thought you two were an item.'

Heather considered for a moment. She was back in Glen's flat, heart pumping wine and adrenalin round her bloodstream, facing the fridge, the two steaks shining out at her. They had seemed to whisper at her and their whisper was seductive. She had picked them up, one in each hand, between shaking fingers. They were cold to touch, but so nearly live flesh. She'd had it in her mind to choose some meat just like this to make her favourite dish – steak tartare – one night. The preparation of it had begun to seep into her tepid, early morning dreams. She would lay the fillet steak carefully on her spotless wooden chopping board, and then slice it into fantastically thin slithers, taking her time, using her best sharp knife so that the meat simply eased apart. She wouldn't bother wiping her fingers, so they would stain red and need scrubbing with hot water before work the next morning. Pepper, salt, and then slip a whole raw egg around the top of the flesh so that it glistened like it was sweating, before bursting the yolk and finishing the dish, raw and perfect.

She had nudged the fridge door closed with her bare shoulder and, no longer worried about her nakedness, squirmed out of her skirt and knickers, leaving smeared trails of blood from the steak to dry on the cream cotton. Steak tartare for one could wait, she thought. She felt she could do anything and that Glen was the one thing she had been waiting for. He must love me, she thought hazily, realizing that this was not necessarily true. She didn't care; she felt frantic, she felt alive, and she felt completely turned on.

When she stumbled back into the bedroom, still cradling the steaks in front of her like offerings to a god, the lights had all expired. As her vision adjusted to the sweaty darkness, she discovered that Glen – still stretched out on the edge of the bed – had completely undressed too. His colourless flesh seemed to get paler and more blotchy as her eyes scanned down his body. His neck and chest were speckled pink and his flat, wide nipples were a light, yellowish peach colour. His stomach was a shade similar to bacon fat, equally flabby. He was snoring and dribbling into the duvet.

Heather clutched the steaks to her chest, scanning curiously as her eyes moved to the shadowy regions past Glen's belly. Rivulets of cherry-coloured, watery blood flowed over her breasts and down her sides and into the feathery, fleshy mound between her legs. Without taking her eyes off Glen's dormant body, Heather slid the steaks down over her own stomach and out across her hips, smearing herself ruby and shimmering, spotting the grey carpet with modern flecks of scarlet which faded to brown. The chill from the fridge had turned her skin taut and the yielding tenderness of the meat clung to it . . .

Heather expelled something between a shout and a sigh and Glen muttered, twisted his sugar stick of a body, and fell off the bed on to the bloodstained floor.

'Heather?' he said. 'Heather, are you there?' He squinted through the darkness. In front of him was a naked woman with her eyes closed and her mouth open. Her flesh had turned a mottled red and was shining. She was swirling what looked like one bloody sponge over her streaming breasts and was easing another gently up her inside leg.

Heather opened her eyes and smiled at Glen. She stretched and, drawing her hands together, offered him two juicy, sparkling steaks.

'Fucking get out of here! You, you complete freak, you bloody pervert. I am not touching those things now. I . . . get out!'

'Oh, Heather, what a shame you two didn't work out. Still, at least you got out and about a bit. You know, I quite fancy this evening class thing myself. What other courses are there?'

'Anything you want, Charlotte. Embroidery. French. Woodwork.' She plucked a college prospectus out of her bag – 'Learning for Life' – and placed it on the coffee table.

'So, are you thinking of some more "adult education" then, Heather?' said Jeff.

'I'm not sure. I do think there's a lot more I could learn. And there's one course next term which does interest me. Who knows, I might take up the twelve-week programme in butchery.'

Crab Head

Andrew Newsham

I have had the thought of cooking the newsagent's head on my mind now for several weeks. Even though the taboo of the subject has dulled considerably, it still persists with the regularity of the dawn chorus. Psychologists would probably be able to provide a hundred different explanations for my strange fancy but I care not for their twisted reasoning. The sickest among them would interpret my thoughts as a latent wish and from this unstable ground turn it into a sexual lust. Only psychologists can put two and two together and get an orgy. In any case, I am not overly concerned; I know there is a vast wilderness of conscience and apathy between thought and action. At heart we are all camels chained to society's oasis and I could no more cook the newsagent's head than I could become prime minister. But then again someone must be the PM.

The newsagent has a face like a lump of dough in which a child has buried a pair of clams and every time I see him he blinks at me suspiciously as if I've just kicked over his rock in some midnight lagoon. To cook his head you would need a very large pan. I've seen the perfect one in Sainsbury's: it has a beautiful heavy-duty wooden handle. Don't worry; I haven't taken measurements.

It used to be the case that I would shrink from the idea when it loomed into my mind in the early morning gloom, but now it's happened so often I'm no longer shocked by it. Self-induced moral indignation only made things worse; the more I chastised myself the more real and exotic the dishes I went on to create. With every censure the thought grew like blood on a blotting pad and it now seems to have taken up permanent residence in my head along with all the other junk.

When I was a boy I could not look at the wallpaper in my Grandma's dining room because skulls watched me from between the petals of the flowers. Of course I realize now it was just a trick of the light, an accidental pattern within a pattern, but once I'd seen them I could not get rid of them. I was quite scared at first. Grandma used to slap my hands with her wooden spoon until I gulped down my food but my eyes held the skulls tight with all the strength of a ship's anchor. I tried everything to get rid of them: closing my eyes, looking only at my food, actually listening to Grandma, but nothing worked. In time they became commonplace, like wallpaper, and I even remember thinking they were a more fitting audience to my grandma's grim commentary on the death of her friends and her own aches and pains than me. After all, I was only twelve and as such unaware of her serious preoccupations. Maybe she'd actually been talking to them. Towards the end she even began to resemble them. As everyone said at the time, we should have buried her earlier.

I bear the man no malice; my thoughts about boiling his head have no basis in any personal hatred. All in all I've barely shared ten words with him in the past two years. We share the perfect relationship in this advanced capitalist society: he is a salesman and I am his customer. There is no bartering or cheery banter about the tabloid women. I buy my cigarettes from him and that is it.

I once heard two old ladies talking about him at the bus stop outside the shop. They both clung to shopping bags, bus passes and the shared belief that he was a martyr. Listening to them, you could not help but agree that it was a shame.

'The things he puts up with!' exclaimed one with indignation.

'He does everything in there and she never lifts a finger,' said the other.

'Well, you know,' the first said, dropping her voice to a whisper, 'she drinks!'

'Really?'

Her voice rose with a quiver of excitement. 'She's in the off licence every day, always a bottle of something, and I know he doesn't drink.'

Her friend tutted. 'It's a shame.'

'She won't even let him go to the pub and he gets the papers at three o'clock every morning.'

'Have you seen how she shouts at him?'

'Oh, I know, it's a shame.'

'And the kids!'

'I know. She expects him to see to them and run the shop. They all treat him like a slave!'

'He has the patience of a saint.'

When the bus came I sat upstairs.

Another time I was waiting for the bus when he was unloading boxes from the back of his car after a trip to the cash and carry. His sons were harassing him for money. Sweating and out of breath – he's very unfit – he was doing his best to unload while ignoring the children. Suddenly, his wife appeared crossly at the shop door in her dressing gown. I'd seen her before so I was already acquainted with the disgust that is permanently etched into her face: a real virago. She looks like one of those portly Russian dolls: inside she goes on for ever, a million carbon copies of her tentacle misery right down to the very last atom.

'Can't you do anything?' she screamed. 'Shut them up! You know I'm trying to sleep!'

He didn't respond. He just calmly put his box down and took out his wallet, offering the boys a £10 note. She swept back inside, utterly disgusted. The boys snatched the money and ran off without so much as a thank you. He shrugged and raised his eyebrows to me in a friendly way as if to involve me in some sort of world-weary kinship. I nodded back my recognition.

Later I regretted having observed the scene and the hapless shrug he had made for my benefit pissed me off. I do not share his implied bondage to life. I am no accomplice to his feckless existence with his fat spoilt children and his fat spoilt wife. In the morning I buy my cigarettes from him and we wish each other well in a polite, unconscious way. Does that involve me in his tragedy?

I don't know when it happened but at some point things changed in my relations with the world. Not so very long ago – well, maybe a few years – people used to smile at me, women used to ask me to light their cigarettes, whenever I got talking to strangers they told me jokes. Lately, however, I have noticed a disturbing trend: complete strangers say things like, 'Don't worry; it might never happen.' Last week in the supermarket an old man with white whiskers and overpowering aftershave told me, 'Don't let the bastards grind you down.' I was only buying cheese. The thing is, I don't recognize myself in the mirror of their eyes. All in all, I'm generally a happy person. Well, as much as anyone is 'happy' without having that crazy religious lobotomy. I have the same blues as everyone and all the normal things: a nice house, a pretty wife, a job that I loathe.

The usual. If anything, it must be the job.

When I get home from work I sometimes feel so sore it's impossible to do anything. I'm very sensitive; sometimes I can't even sleep. I work for the social security, only it's not so much a job as a sick kind of game. Every day it's the same shapes, the same patterns. They crawl up to my desk with borrowed flesh blinking in the sunshine, scratching with tooth decay and worrying where the next fag will come from. They bumble about in a fog, their eyes crusted with sleepy routine. I think, 'Is this really life, is that your life?'

On no account am I allowed to give any advice that might be helpful. Their ignorance is a cornerstone of society, to be quantified by armies of bureaucratic clerks in the grip of some kind of brain fever. I once hung a sign on the notice board: 'They must be maintained in the misery to which they have become accustomed!' No one saw it; it was soon covered by second-hand car adverts. In this enlightened age I get them to fill out forms, then I fill out more forms, dealing with the futile movements of small change. As I go through the motions the world keeps turning, the same shapes, the same patterns, skulls smiling through the roses.

I am not a violent man, but although it seems like a very evil thing to contemplate, I have thought about how it would happen. It's a kind of dream. On a perfectly ordinary morning I will wake as usual at seven and wash and shave and make toast while drinking coffee and climbing into my suit. My mornings are always such a clutter of action. Walking my usual route to work, I light my first cigarette and the taste of Marlboro bites sweetly into my tongue. Everything is still and, as I round the corner on to Dogpool Lane by the scrapyard, I notice the street sign has been vandalized again. Once again some wit has run off with the 'L'. Somehow, though, it seems to fit. As I walk up the lane the newsagent's comes into view, its windows radiating a yellow chip-pan glow. Pershore Road is the usual logjam. Although the cars aren't going anywhere fast and you could easily walk between the bumpers, I don't dare risk it and walk up the road to the school crossing.

When I enter the shop to buy my cigarettes the newsagent greets me with his customary 'hello' and reaches for my daily pack. Relations pass as usual: simple, polite conversation as I fumble through my wallet for change. Then, as I hand him my money, he calmly suggests that I cook his head. He asks me very matter of factly, as if telling me the weather report for the day, and I flinch in recognition of the social impropriety of the request, but only just so.

'I'm sure you won't use too much salt,' he jokes, taking the awkwardness out of the situation. I laugh and he leads me through the beaded curtains into the back room.

I use a small guillotine for the decapitation. On a large table in the centre of the room he has gathered almost every ingredient and utensil I could possibly need. There is even a fondue kit with a picture on the box showing a Swedish family sitting around a lobotomized skull, having a whale of a time with the fondue forks. It is the moment of truth. Head in hand, I have to decide what to do. All is going smoothly except there is no cheese grater. NO FUCKING CHEESE GRATER. Can you believe it? One of the most standard and useful kitchen utensils ever invented and the useless fuckwit was more interested in making sure the fucking Education section was in the motherfucking *Guardian*. Holding his bloody head in my hands, I rush and kick his bulky lifeless trunk again and again until I lose my breath.

Slowly I regain my cool.

When I am calm I choose how to cook him. I almost opt for the traditional roast; the finishing touch, of course, would be an apple in the mouth, but this is mere fancy. His head will have to be boiled like a lobster. The oven sits in the corner. It is an unremarkable sixties model that could do with a clean but is otherwise adequate. On the opposite side of the room a table is neatly set for the meal. Threading a needle, I sew his eyelids closed to prevent his eyeballs popping in the water and place the head into the large pan from Sainsbury's. As I suspected, it is the perfect size. I fill the pan at the sink and place it on the biggest ring on the hob. The water boils in about six minutes and I add salt, saffron and nutmeg and let it simmer for about half an hour. After ten minutes the head starts to scream like Jimmy Somerville singing the opening yelp of the Sylvester hit 'I Feel Love'. It only lasts for a few minutes but it's enough to get the song stuck in my crop. 'Oooooo, I feel love, I feel love, I feel love, I feel love, I FEEL LOVE.'

While I'm waiting for the head to finish, I try to fold a napkin into a rose in the fancy way they do in expensive restaurants. After several attempts I give up and settle for an aeroplane. I then drain the water, unpick his eyes and serve the head on a plate. The blood which covers the floor in a thick puddle is getting sticky and I am glad to finally light the candle on the table, bang the dinner gong and get out of the place.

I have speculated about who will eat the dish. Instinct tells me it will be enjoyed by the newsagent's wife, and, of course, the thousand miniature wives within her. Even though I have explored the entirety of this fantasy – police conviction, extra unexpected guests, an appearance on *Ready Steady Cook* – I can no more stop thinking about it than he can stop being a sphere of dough with oysters for eyes. We are both to blame and, at the same time, we are both hapless victims of fate.

For some strange reason I just know his head will taste oddly of crab.

An Essay on the Potential of Torture in the Home

Edward Scrivens

Raymond Burke watched the fox as it tentatively nosed its way across the concrete drive of the house in front of him, picked out in the hostile glow of a security light. It was nosing around a dustbin – one of the new green ones. Ray felt a pang of empathy with it – it obviously expected to be caught any minute; perhaps it felt that the prize was worth the risk. Bit like him, really.

Gritting his teeth, Ray tore his attention away from the fox, and back to the job in hand. You're stalling, man, he thought. Don't put it off; just get in there, do it. Crossing the road in quick, long strides, Ray stepped on to the drive of the house. The fox looked at him reproachfully and ran. He carried on. He knew from careful observation that he must avoid the wobbly flagstone near the thistle patch if he wanted to remain undetected. This obstacle negotiated, he reached the wall of the house without further incident. The old man would be fast asleep in bed by now – doped up to the eyeballs on sleeping pills. The alarm wasn't working, as he well knew, so there was no excuse for any delay. Deep down he was just putting it off. He was scared. Of one old man. Or perhaps because this old man represented his return to crime. His heart pounding and his mouth dry, he slipped down the side passage, pulling the crowbar out of his jacket pocket as he neared the loose window. A swift crack later, the window swung open, and Ray was inside.

Upstairs, the decrepit form of Gerald McAuley was wracked by a cough. Spluttering awake, Gerald reached for the glass of water at the bedside. Cursing his reluctance to take the sleeping pills, Gerald felt the last vestiges of sleep fall away, leaving him feeling more alert than he did most of the day. Typical. Sitting up in bed, his blanket falling away from toast-rack ribs, he considered his next move. He could either lie there and wait for sleep to reclaim him – not a likely occurrence, now he was coughing – or he could get up and go sit in the lounge. Swivelling out of bed, he pulled on his slippers – a nice cup of cocoa and the telly would soon sort him out. Hobbling out of the room, he crossed the landing to his stair lift and sat down, letting the whirring motor do the job his legs would once have done.

Ray had climbed into the bathroom, he realized. The scent of floral talcum powder was thick in the air. Shaking his head and trying not to cough, Ray struggled to remember the lay-out of the house; he'd tried to imprint it on his brain when he'd called earlier in the week. The bedroom was on the first floor, the stairs were to the left, as you came out of the bath-room. Confident now, Ray opened the door. The hinge squeaked, followed by a terrible crack, like a gunshot. Ray froze.

Gerald hummed quietly to himself as he rummaged for the cocoa. His mind began to wander, and for a moment he was back reliving the battles in his past. A gunshot. He jerked – that wasn't a Nip, that was the bathroom door – someone was in the house. Gerald felt the familiar heat of adrenalin kick in. If this was another burglar . . . His blood boiled with anger – twice in a month – and just because his pension didn't stretch to repairing the alarm. His body drew itself up, falling into long-lost patterns of action. Chemical power sloshed through his system, strengthening, rejuvenating. Before he knew what he was doing, he had scooped up the heaviest saucepan and was moving towards the door.

No one came to investigate, and after a short time Ray began to relax. He moved further into the hallway, past the kitchen door, and then drew level with the lounge door, which stood open on to shadow. The stairs were dimly visible ahead – the old coot must have left a light on. Just the thing to help a burglar; how thoughtful of him. All of a sudden Ray felt uneasy – someone was close by, and he was in danger. He swivelled, looking for the source of this unease, but found nothing. Relax, man, he told himself, you're jumping at draughts. The saucepan caught him full in the face, and he crumpled.

His arms aching from the swing, Gerald grinned – the burglar was out for the count, face down on the floor. Now – to business. Tie him up, then ring the police. They hadn't managed to solve the last burglary, so this time he'd give them the culprit on a plate. Thinking hard, he decided on washing line – the plastic-covered sort – to tie Ray up with. Slipping back into the kitchen, he pulled out his coil of washing line from under the sink – you didn't dare leave it outside, or the local vandals would nick it. Dragging Ray through to the tiny dining room, with more than a little difficulty, Gerald flicked on the light. At the sight of the burglar's face, he swore.

'Bastard, you fuckin' bastard,' he spat. Lying on the floor in front of him was the man from the clinic who had called a week ago, and to whom he had shown the – oh, of course – the money. Never one to trust a bank, Gerald, like many of his generation, had hoarded his money under the mattress. And there was rather a lot of it. Easily enough to tempt a reformed thief, who was now working as a healthcare volunteer. Gerald felt the hate begin to boil in his gut. He'd let this man into his home, trusted him, and been betrayed. What had the world come to, when simple old-fashioned trust was a liability? Kicking out with his slippered foot, Gerald rolled the thief over on to his stomach again, so as to conceal that treacherous face, that vessel of deceit. At that moment, Gerald decided that he wasn't going to call the police. They'd only let him go again – let him do this to other people, maybe others without his skills. Convinced that he could no longer allow this man to run free and terrorize innocent people, and with the justice of what he was doing burnt into his mind, Gerald began to truss Ray to one of the tough wooden dining chairs.

Ray groaned, his head swimming. Slowly he forced his eyes open. He registered Gerald standing over him. He groaned, realizing that he had been caught. The fact that he was tied to a chair began to worm its way into his consciousness. His first thought was that he couldn't afford to go to jail. It would have to be the drunk act then.

'Whassha matter wi my eyes? Why'm I tied up?'

The old man slapped him, open palmed. 'You know why, you bastard. You'm 'ere for the money, aren't you?'

'What money? I was at a party –'

'Party?' The old man didn't sound convinced.

'Yeah – got 'ome, an' me door wouldn't open, so went in through the window, day I?'

'You're trying to tell me you thought this was your house, boy?'

'Shiiit. Ain't it?'

Gerald swung a heavy punch, rocking Ray back on his seat and splitting his lip. Blood started to dribble.

'Listen to me. I know why you're here, and I know I ain't going to let you get away with it.'

'You're going to call the cops?'

'Oh, no.' Gerald shook his head, the light momentarily dancing off his large bald patch. 'The police don't care about us. They just leave us to look after ourselves. So I'm going to do the world a favour. Fix it so you never steal again.'

Fear twisted inside Ray's stomach – the man sounded mad, absolutely raving.

'What? What are you –'

'What am I going to do? Have you ever seen a film of Japanese torture? No? Well, it doesn't matter, you'll soon see what I mean.'

And with that he turned, and left Ray alone in the room.

As soon as he was out of sight, Ray started to struggle, wrenching his bonds this way and that, pushing for a weak spot. His wrists were his best bet but it wasn't looking good. Subsiding, Ray closed his eyes, trying to think his way out of this mess. If the old guy was telling the truth and he wasn't to be handed over to the police, then there must be some use for him here. Unless . . . but Ray blocked that thought quickly. Old men don't kill people, do they? He had said something about torture but how would he do that? Sweat sprang to his brow and to the palms of his hands. Sensing an escape route, Ray began to smear his wrists with sweat, ignoring the burning from the abrasions. Desperately he tugged at the bonds again, but they still refused to give. The door creaked open and Gerald entered, a tray in his hand, on which rested a kettle, three or four knives, a box of matches and a mug of cocoa. Ray suddenly realized how the old man intended to torture him. He wet himself.

Gerald had gone into the kitchen after he left the dining room with every intention of finishing off his cup of cocoa.

Filling the kettle and switching it on, he ladled cocoa powder into a cup and considered what to do about the thief. For all his bravado, Gerald really hadn't decided, only that the police were no longer an option – that it was time the responsible members of the community took a stand. However, what that stand was going to be, he had, as yet, no idea.

The idea of torture had seemed preposterous when it came out of his mouth, but suddenly it seemed all too logical. All of the people he had known in the army who had been tortured had been irreparably changed by the experience, which was exactly what he wanted to happen here. So – the question now became – how to torture him? Knives were an option of course, he had plenty of those. In fact, he thought, he might as well get them ready while he waited for his cocoa. Sliding a tray out from its rack, he pulled three knives out of the block – a large butcher's carving knife, a small, serrated knife and a larger, curved cheese knife. After a second's thought, he added an apple peeler as well. Stepping over to the kettle, he tutted to see that it had still not boiled. Twisting the lid, he opened it. A cloud of steam burst out, scorching his hand. Jumping back, Gerald grinned – a second idea. Pouring water over the cocoa powder, he added the half-full kettle to the tray. As an afterthought he added a box of matches. Then he left the kitchen.

Placing the tray on the table, Gerald turned back to Ray.

'You might have worked this out. I'm going to torture you – to teach you the error of your ways.'

'You can't! It's illegal. You're absolutely mad.'

Gerald ignored him and turned to the tray.

'Don't ignore me, you bastard! You can't do this.'

Gerald swept up the carving knife and sliced into Ray's cheek. Ray screamed. At first, there was nothing, just a dry wound, but slowly blood began to ebb from the wound, faster and faster, pumping out, to mingle with the tears streaming from Ray's eyes.

'You cut me,' Ray cried, hysteria in his voice. 'You cut me, you bastard you cut me . . .'

Gerald merely smiled, pleased at the effect his treatment was having. Perhaps he should go public with it. But no. Others might not understand the necessity of it.

'You cut me, you cut me, oh God, you cut me . . .'

The man's babbling was starting to become tedious. Gerald felt irritation build, like an itch. Eventually, there was only one way to scratch it. Raising the kettle, Gerald swung it into Ray's head. The babbling ceased.

'Better. Now we have to show the world what you are. Can't have you sneaking up on anyone else.'

Taking another piece of washing line, Gerald moved round to the back of Ray. He passed the spare length through Ray's arms and yanked, forcing them back, inflating Ray's chest to its fullest extent.

Returning to the front again, Gerald tore open Ray's shirt front, and picked up the knife. He began to carve deep grooves in Ray's flesh. As he worked, he whistled. Eventually he stopped, and stepped back to survey his handiwork. He tutted in annoyance – the cuts were obscured by the chest hair. Immediately he had a brainwave. Moving to the downstairs bathroom, he returned with a razor and shaving foam, which he proceeded to daub over Ray's bloodstained chest – the foam turning pink as he did so. Sloshing a little of the now warm water from the kettle over the foam, Gerald worked up a lather, and then proceeded to shave off the hair in neat strips. Time to show the boy his masterpiece, Gerald mused. Pulling up the left eyelid, Gerald dribbled a little warm water from the kettle into the eye. Ray awoke with a yelp. The corners of Gerald's mouth twitched in satisfaction.

'Look down.'

Ray let his head flop down. Better to appear co-operative, he thought helplessly, maybe the pain – oh God, the pain – would stop. On his chest, in deep cuts, he read THIEF. He screamed – a brutally primal sound, harking back to the days when our ancestors were mauled by sabre-toothed tigers.

Outside, the fox howled in sympathy.

Green

Jackie Gay

– Come on, said Rosa. – Let's get out of here.

I was lying on the floor listening to Neil Young. *Hey hey, my my. Rock and Roll can never die.* As long as my eyes were closed I could keep up with the wishing. Wishing I was a singer: funky, like Chrissie Hynde; or an actress, a proper one, winning Emmys and Oscars for my gutsy portrayals. Wishing for love. If I opened them there was only the iron-shaped burn on the carpet next to my head, the pale green swirly carpet that made us feel seasick when we were drunk. The landlord would have us about it sooner or later.

– Come on, Jo. She was shaking my shoulder. – Let's go out.

– With what? I said, from behind my lids. – Monopoly money?

– I'll borrow some from her upstairs. She's always got money.

– Go on then, I said, rolling over. There was fluff under the sofa, bits of string hanging down where the cat had got at it. – Twist my arm.

We didn't go to our local, backstreet pub that could have

been in anytown; but the flashy new one on the sea front. There was a drinks promotion, two for the price of one, or so we'd heard. We could see it as we walked down Sea Road, throbbing and glistening, the last building before the beach, music beating out in waves. It seemed odd – a bit of a fake, somehow – those lights and music when it wasn't even properly dark yet. The sun was still hanging in the sky, cut in half by the sea, the night creeping up to cover it.

– Jesus, it's heaving, said Rosa, when we got inside.

It smelt of packed bodies, beer, a whiff of brine through the open windows.

– Grockles, I said scornfully, although I was one too, just down for the summer, to work, get a bit of sun. – They should have a special bar for people who *live* here.

– They should that, he said, his voice a soft burr. – Can I get you something?

My mouth wouldn't work.

– Vodka, said Rosa, large ones. We'll share a tonic.

I nodded. His eyes were holding mine.

– Anything you wish for, he said.

And suddenly I was glad that the pub was packed. That I got jostled towards him, towards his body. Streams of people were still pushing their way in, forcing us back to the wall. We had to turn our heads sideways to drink – great thirsty gulps – then swivel back so we could look at each other again, nose to nose. I was as tall as him, could look straight into his green eyes. Jewel green. Green pines after rain.

– Let's get out of here, said Rosa.

– Why? I said. Danny's arm was round my waist, steadying himself. That was his name. Danny. Daniel.

I looked at her and then at him, and we all knew, even then.

– That's the only trouble with him, I said to Rosa a couple of weeks later, feeling the urge to talk about him. – Keeps to his own timetable, doesn't he? I was sunk into the sofa, staring at the mildewing ceiling. I couldn't seem to keep myself straight any more. My spine felt like it was made out of rubber and I was most relaxed horizontal. Danny liked that, his lip curled up and his big hands reached out to me.

She looked up from her novel. – The only trouble? she said.

– Yeah. You know . . . staying up night after night and then disappearing for days.

– We hardly keep regular hours ourselves, said Rosa.

That was true. Working in pubs and nightclubs, going to the beach for dawn, sleeping all day until the low afternoon sun poked through our window and woke us; sweat-sheened, thirsty. We'd find presents from Danny on the back step. Apple juice. Bread, eggs, the *Mirror*; twenty Embassy sometimes. He'd go into the corner shop and raid the shelves for us. The old Irishman behind the counter used to laugh. – You fattening those girls up for something, he'd say, and Danny would say – Ach, they're so scatty, can't be trusted to feed themselves. Shouldn't be away from their mothers really . . .

He told me all this. He liked to tell me what he'd done for me.

When we were going out I'd skive off work and come back to the flat early – the shadowed green of the room like a woodland clearing after the bright noon sun outside. I'd pour oils into the bath and fill the room with steam and watch the windowsill ferns sway like seaweed as billows rose from the water. I'd lie there for hours thinking of nothing, dreaming, suspended; and then pull the plug and feel the water slip out slowly from underneath my skin, damming sections with my shoulders and hips and then setting them loose suddenly to gush and gurgle when I finally rose. Then I'd play Neil Young again. *Once I thought I saw you, in a crowded sleazy bar. Dancing on the night from star to star.* It could make me cry sometimes, the beauty of it. Rosa came in and found me sitting cross-legged on the floor, weeping. I was staring at the carpet, the colour of new shoots, so delicate and fresh and fragile, tracing my fingers around the patterns.

The landlord called it avocado when he was trying to rent us the place.

– Avocado carpets and avocado bathroom suite, he said, pushing out his chest, like it was a palace.

– Not for long, said Rosa, under her breath. – Not if we've got anything to do with it.

– What was that, girls? said the landlord.

– Nothing. We smiled at him. Tweedledee and Tweedledum. We thought we could get away with anything.

– Any chance of a discount? said Rosa.

Danny laughed at our landlord. Knew him from way back, when they were kids growing up on these streets tucked back from the sea frontages, out of the way of the tourists. Bought cheap houses and did them out cheap and only rented them to girls. Girls'll always pay, our landlord bragged in his local, apparently. In the front room there was a woman with two kids and a pregnant dog. Upstairs the lass who always had money but never cracked her eyelids before lunchtime. We were in the back room, the old outhouse our avocado bathroom.

– He won't overcharge you now, Danny said. That was one of his tricks. Let you get settled and working and then put the rent up. – I've made sure of that. He looked pleased with himself. Danny liked getting things sorted. We were grateful, felt like we had an ally in this strange town of cash-in-hand and fortnight breaks and refugees from the north. From coldwetcities to sparkling beaches and cliff-top palm trees and skinny dipping in the emerald sea at dawn. It was paradise sometimes. It was to me, as I lay languid on the sofa, waiting for Danny, surrounded by greenery, lush in the evening sun. I'd told him I liked plants and he'd brought round a pallet full. A mini-tropics on the back step when I woke from my afternoon's dreaming.

He told me he was married on my twenty-first birthday.

We were sitting at the bar drinking cheap fizz. I felt my stool wobble and looked to the floor to see if it had shifted. Laughter was too loud; glasses vibrated on the counter.

– I was really young, said Danny. – You know how these things are. I wish I wasn't but I can't carry on lying to you, Jo.

He looked pleadingly at me. He expected me to do something – comfort him maybe, say yes Danny, how awful for you. It's OK, it's OK. Water rushed in my ears, hot and sulphurous. For a second I thought my fontanelle might burst – up into the air, like a volcano plug popping under pressure – and let all my hot, lethal lava out.

He was still going on. He was drunk.

– She won't let me go, he said. – She's got a thing for me. You know, like a stalker or something. And then there's all her family. They're everywhere in this town. I'd never get work again.

I watched his mouth moving around his face like a puppet's. His jaw was slack and deep ridges had appeared on his brow as he leant towards me, willing me to understand. I wanted to smooth them out. Stroke his face. Knead and mould and pummel it back into one that had no veneer; that had never lied.

– That means he does this all the time, said Rosa. – Have affairs.

– You never liked him, I spat, lashing out. – Look what he's done for us. Tears fizzed on my hot cheeks.

– Yeah, and now we know *why*.

Rosa goes out with bookish blokes, too thin, the sort who want to *talk* to you. At least Danny never bothered too much about that. Well, only sometimes when he'd eye me with a glint – see if I was up for it – and then reach down into his deep pockets and draw out his spatulate fingers, iced with speed, and I'd suck them and we'd jabber nonsense for hours. Go on adventures in the botanical gardens. – Yeah, yeah. I know what you mean, we'd say, never finishing a sentence, running till our hearts thumped out of our chests. And then we'd turn the bed into a boat on the green sea and sail jauntily off into sexland. – You're nuts, he'd say, tapping the side of my head fondly as I hauled in the jib sheets. – Got rocks in your head.

I loved him by then. By my twenty-first.

– What are you going to do then? said Rosa, after a while. The room was gloomy, like the inside of an empty wine bottle. For the first time since coming south I felt cold.

– Come on, I said. – Let's get out of here.

We went to the local and our landlord was in there, with his brother, laughing expansively and buying everyone drinks. People must have heard he was there, came in specially for a freebie.

– Where's Danny? he said.

I couldn't work out if the sneer on his face – a rise of lip and cheek, a mocking eye – had always been there or if I was just seeing it now. I resented this, the whole world changing because Danny was married.

– Fuck Danny, I said, taking my Pils out of his hand. – And fuck you.

– She's upset, said Rosa, standing at the bar with them. I sat in a corner and examined the lino, watched blokes playing darts, tried to shut myself down. There was still noise in my head, rushing in my ears like the sound inside shells.

Even here, a mile back from the beach, there was sand on the floor and my foot scraped on it, grinding it, making it smaller, diminishing it until it finally turned to dust. Then suddenly Rosa grabbed my shoulder and hauled me through the hangers-on and out of the door.

– What? I said. – What's going on?

Rosa hooked her arm through mine, hurried me down the street. – You were hardly having the time of your life in there.

– Yeah but . . . I never even finished my beer.

– It's him. And his brother. She pulled me closer to her. – I think they've got plans for us.

I went topless sunbathing on the beach, told Rosa I was sick of the white triangles, it'd make me feel whole again if I got brown all over. But a photographer arrived from the local paper, leering and snapping, and a reporter asking questions, saying there were otherplaces for people like me, didn't I realize this was a family beach?

– How would you feel if your boyfriend was married? I said, hoping for one mad moment that he'd print this and she'd read it: Danny's wife.

The reporter's pen hovered over a notebook; his eyes stayed on my chest. – A girl like you shouldn't have to worry about that too much, he said. – And anyway, he's not your boyfriend if he's married, is he?

When the paper came out there was nothing about Danny, only a smudgy photograph with half my face missing and an editorial about this being England. It's not the SouthofFrance, you know.

– How could you do this to me? said Danny, appearing on the back step in a cloud of rage. – Flaunting yourself for everyone to see.

I laughed. – How could *I* do this to *you*? A tiny moment of triumph. Half a second or so. But I didn't want to triumph over Danny. I wanted him to be mine.

– You're just asking for trouble, doing things like that, he said.

Crack. I slapped his face and it sounded like lightning; my arm had moved so fast it should have been burning. We both stared at it, limp and hanging from my shoulder.

– Jesus, Jo.

– Leave her, I said.

– I can't. It's complicated. You don't understand.

– You should have told me. I wouldn't have let it go this far. You should never have come near me, should have stayed at home with *her*.

– Should I have? said Danny. – Would you not?

The next day I found a peace lily on the back step. Some vitamin C, teabags, jam and soft rolls. Rosa and I wolfed them; we didn't have any money, hadn't been working much.

– You shouldn't take stuff off him still, she said, her mouth smeared with sticky redness, her fingers flicking over the pages of her book.

– No, I said. – We'd better get to work then.

– Shame, said Rosa. – I'm just getting to a good bit.

The hall was filled with landlord. – Girls! he said, smarmily, opening his arms as if we were supposed to leap into them giggling. – Where are you two off to?

– Work, said Rosa.

– Work, I said.

He eyed us. – On a beautiful day like this? Thought you'd be out sunning yourselves. Topping up the tan. He had a newspaper stuffed in his back pocket and the carpet and wall lurched to one side as I realized that my tits were probably in there somewhere.

We shrugged. – Gotta pay the rent, said Rosa.

– Plenty of ways to do that, said the landlord. – Plenty of ways for girls like you to make a bit of green.

The lass upstairs said she'd started by doing photographs for him and now, well, she did a bit more, you know. She had long pale hair which fell over her face and she looked at us through this mist. Her room was lovely. Sunny and bright and high up. You could just see the sea twitching in the distance if you stood on tiptoe and looked out over the houses and shops and long slope down to the beach. I could see why she didn't want to leave it, go back to coldplace, poorville; where there was no sparkle, no horizon.

His wife came into the bar where I was working and told me to leave off. She had rings up to her knuckles and twisted them as she spoke. – We've got history, me and Danny, she said. – You know nothing about him.

I wondered if it was something heroic, like she'd saved Danny's life, nursed him through some debilitating illness; but decided it was more likely something messy and human. Shared debts. Family obligations. Oh, yes, and the fact that she loved him. Her eyes swept the bar and me, snagging on my bare shoulders, my tanned legs, which had gone empty and cold inside.

– You won't last, she said, her voice rising in her throat.

– You needn't have come then, I said. – Why bother?

– To let you know, she said. – You won't last and I will.

Jealousy stripped my blood of its redness. My knees crumbled beneath me and I had to grip the counter, watch my fingers go white and start to slide. She left.

– He's put the rent up, said Rosa when I got home. I felt the lava in my head wobble again. – Didn't waste any time, did he?

– We're not paying it, right? I said. – Just don't give him anything.

– He wants us to do some photos; glamour, he says.

– Yeah, and I was born yesterday.

– I think it was your tits that set him off.

– That was a stupid thing to do.

Rosa shrugged. – Everyone makes mistakes, she said.

We started going out around the town, to the flashier bars, the late night clubs where the local boys pick up new women, just landed in seasidetown. Danny was around but we didn't talk to him, didn't talk to anyone much except each other. Instead we laughed and flirted and hitched our skirts up as we twisted on the bar stools. Sometimes I could see Danny operating, his shiny face without a crack in it, his hands; imagine his soft voice smoothing over the edges of nervous girls' chatter. There was something too smooth about him, too soft and lulling, like the last fizz of the sea on the beach before the tide turns. But it worked. Girls loved him; their necks craned when he walked past, they danced around him, stumbling on their heels. His artifice was practised, subconscious. – What can I do? he'd say to his mates, turning his white palms to the sky. – They just fall at my feet.

He caught me on the way to the loo once. – You want to watch it, he said. – You two are getting a reputation.

– For what? I said, wide-eyed. – *Not* sleeping around?

– Just watch it, Jo, he said.

The landlord rapped on our door and we answered it sleepily, sweetly, promising money; acting vague, incompetent. He must have heard something about us because he turned up in the club that night and watched us dally with each other at the bar. We were becoming quite a spectacle. The landlord got terribly excited and made frames with his hands and clicking noises with his teeth as if we were in a photo session. He wrote febrile notes and shoved them under our door and stopped asking for the rent. Rosa took the plants upstairs and I went to the train station to book tickets out of showtown.

Danny was out in the street playing football with some lads. He lived in the road next to the station. I remembered this as I got near there, knew why I'd volunteered to go.

– Which is your house? I said. – Is she in?

There were other blokes out too: dads, brothers; fixing cars and hanging around lampposts and kicking the ball up and down the hot street. Danny waved at a block and I tried to guess which one was his, what it was like inside. What albums he had and whether the kitchen was clean. Spotless, I guessed.

– She's cooking, he said. – Likes me out of the way. Anyway, you know me, can't stand to be inside.

This was true: rooms shrank around Danny; a pub was about as domesticated as he got.

– Where are you going, anyway?

I nodded at the station. A train pulled out, stirring up dust in its wake.

Danny grabbed my hand and shoved it in his pocket. – One more night, he purred in my ear, before the dust cleared. – Are you up for it?

Out on the headland we stared at the glassy sea. We could hear it moving though; swelling and breathing and sucking energy invisibly, under the surface. I felt that if I wanted to I could release it, the wildness, maybe send a tidal wave galloping over the promenade, whose lights we could see, strung out below us. Sweep away the beach huts, the pretendhomes, the bullshit, and leave a clean wide sweep of sand, glittering, instead. Danny built a fire and we inched closer to it, drawing our world inwards until there was nothing else but our faces, the flickering fire and the muffled boom of the ocean.

– I love it up here, said Danny. – Used to come here all the time when we were kids. It was ourplace.

– What, you and our landlord? I said. – I bet he was a pleasant child.

– I don't suppose you've paid him? said Danny, exasperated.

– No, but we're arranging a threesome tomorrow night to settle our debt.

His face wrinkled. – Don't talk like that. I don't know what you and Rosy think you've been up to lately. He called her Rosy; he liked her, liked us. Our erratic finances and poor eating habits. How he could drive past in the dead of night and see our light on and find us playing cards on the sticky green carpet, laughing and hiccuping and falling over on the way to the avocado bathroom, our sea legs failing us. Upping and leaving hometown one day because the sun was shining and heat on concrete made us restless. I thought he might even miss us.

– Well, I said, can you think of a better way to wind the boys of this town up?

We dozed on each other's shoulders. Danny murmured something in his sleep. It could have been *I love you, Jo.* I made it that, in my head. When I stirred next we were curled and warm in the grass, the noise from the sea had stopped and the ferment in my head had quietened too. Danny pulled me close to him, fierce in his sleepiness.

– I fucking love you, I heard him say.

We had to sneak our stuff out of the flat, out the back and along the alley. The lass from upstairs helped us pack.

– You'll have to be quiet, she said. – He's got spies all along the street.

– Spies? said Rosa.

– You're kidding, I said.

She looked me straight in the eyes. – I'm not, she said. – That's why I'm helping you. There's not many get one over on him.

– You come too, I said, but she had already turned away

and walked up to her attic room, her tower with its view.

Rosa tugged at my shirt and we left, running swiftly through the back streets as the dawn light touched the sea behind us. The train was on the platform and we jumped on it, slamming the heavy door and sitting down, panting, laughing, willing the engine to start and the carriages begin to creak out of hisplace. His place. Then Rosa's eyes grew wide and she clutched my arm, pointing out our landlord's bulk growing on the platform, red-faced and steaming.

But the train was already moving and only his words could catch us. – Oi! You two! he yelled. – Where d'you think you're going? You owe me *money*.

We waved, blew kisses.

– There's plenty more where you came from, he roared, a torn edge to his voice as the train picked up speed. – Go back to your fucking Bull Ring. See if I care.

I looked for marks of Danny on my skin. I felt like he must be there; smudges, bruises, fine indelible scars lacing across my body. But there was nothing. My skin was smooth, clean, brown. There was nothing visible. Back in Brum they would only say, Gotta nice tan while you were there then, why did you come back? We hadn't worked out what we were going to say about that yet. They wouldn't believe us if we said we were homesick. We'd sent exuberant postcards, messages from easystreet. Even boasted about how many men there were, all with money, and how we could smell the sea from our back door.

That was it. I could still smell him. Breathe deeply into my cupped hands and it was still there, like an echo just fading. Brine and bodies and a whiff of risk. And I wondered if I would ever just fall like that again. Into someone's eyes, so green; and, as the train moved on through bleached grass edged with ruby poppies, I wished – just once more – that I could.

Ringers

Rob Smith

Paul glanced at himself again in the rear-view mirror. It was one of those extra long curved ones that taxi drivers use, with a fringe of gold-coloured tassels that were still swinging slightly from when they'd climbed in. Yeah. He could pass for seventeen, no problem. He turned to Zaf who was watching him and grinning. 'Are you sure your uncle isn't going to mind?'

'Mind, spar? Course he's not. He's not even going to *know* if you get this rust bucket moving some time in the next twenty-four hours.'

Paul scowled at his friend. 'This is no rust bucket, Zaf. This car's a classic. Ever since I first met your uncle, I've been dying to take it out for a spin. A Cortina Mark Two 1600E! When this was brand new, it would have turned heads, I can tell you.'

Zaf pushed in the cigarette lighter knob on the dash. 'It still does turn heads. But that's mainly because there's a hole in the back box and it sounds like a rocket-fuelled fart trapped in a biscuit tin.' His unlit cigarette dipped and nodded in his mouth as he spoke.

Paul checked himself in the rear-view mirror again. Did he look old enough? 'You don't think we'll get stopped, do you?'

'Come on! A five-minute spin round the block?' said Zaf. The lighter knob showed no sign of popping out and he tugged it free of its socket, looking dispiritedly at the cold, grey element. '*Blud claat*,' he said scornfully. 'Now if it was a Porsche or a Mercedes, we might. But have you ever heard of the police stopping a black man driving a dinosaur like this? Got to be kidding. They're not going to be jealous of *this*, now are they?'

Paul turned the key in the ignition and heard the engine thunder into life. 'It's noisy but really, there's nothing wrong with this car that a bit of tender loving care wouldn't fix.'

'Holy Musa! The way you talk about cars! It's a conveyance, man – takes you from A to B, hopefully without the assistance of the RAC. I mean, to hear you go on about those ringers the way you do, anyone would think them murdering people rather than just dismantling cars.'

'I know,' Paul replied, reversing cautiously towards the entry. 'It's just they don't even *see* the cars they tear up, they don't value them or treat them with any respect. It's like ripping a book to pieces so you can sell off the pages one at a time. A car's more than that.'

'Don't tell me – each car's got an identity. Even a bottom of the range Y reg. Datsun Cherry!' Zaf hooked his Zippo from his shirt pocket and lit up.

Paul laughed. 'Yeah, well. I might draw the line a bit before then. It's just that to those guys, whatever the car is, they rip it apart. I don't like that.' Crackling over some broken glass, he checked up and down the road for passing pandas, then swung the car out into the street.

There had been six in the space of four weeks. The first had appeared at the beginning of the summer, a brand new Ford with a small hole in the windscreen on the passenger side. It just might have been a write-off; maybe there was some damage Paul couldn't see. Apart from the hole it looked gleaming. The three men completed the job in just a couple of days. The bumpers – big plastic mouldings sprayed the same metallic blue as the rest of the car – were removed first, then the interior over the course of the next day. The bonnet, the window glass, the doors all followed. The parts were stacked in the back of an old Transit to be shipped off to one of the many local scrapyards. Or on to another car in some backstreet garage somewhere. The skeleton that remained was hauled on to the back of the blue and white tow truck by a winch with a hook heavy enough to drag a railway carriage. The first car was still recognizable when the tow truck came for it. But later, with the fourth and fifth, older cars demanding less respect, the whine of an angle grinder announced the final stage of their destruction. Not bothering with goggles, one of the men would spray fountains of sparks from each of the roof struts until the top was sitting awkwardly on the body of the car like an ill-fitting tin lid.

Ringers. That's what the papers called them. It was simply another word for thieves. And some were conducting their business just three doors down from him. Paul, who at only sixteen had already learnt to drive and was a self-confessed car fanatic, could not help but keep an eye on them.

To start with there were several weeks between each car. The first was the Ford, then there was a Renault, an old Toyota, a Sierra, a Prelude, a Metro then another Ford. The same three men dealt with each. The large wrestler with a thick neck and tattoos on his heavy forearms drove the tow truck. The small one, dark and shifty eyed, spent most of his time under the bonnets. Then there was the one whose yard it was, a man with a wiry moustache and thick red hair who crammed his rangy frame into the cabs and stripped them. They might have different areas of specialization but they had a common purpose. Following the initial drive over the summer, business ceased. Probably for good. The last car was simply wheeled out of the yard in the night into a side road and a rag shoved in the petrol tank and lit. They didn't seem too concerned about covering their tracks. Having said that, a large spring lying in a pool of oil was the only other evidence that anything had been happening in that yard at all.

With each car Paul asked himself the same questions. Should the police be told? Did he have any loyalty to the men? After all, it might be the car of a relative or friend next. The other neighbours must have known what was going on too, but they were doing nothing, so if anyone was going to act it would have to be him. But another voice took the ringers' side. Times were hard, they were just making a living. Insurance companies covered the cost of replacement in any case. Then there was the unwritten code, the common understanding between people in the area when it came to contact with uniformed law; nothing to do with me.

He kept Zaf, his mate across the way, informed of every development. 'God man, this is a crime syndicate,' he said as Zaf angled his face, admiring his profile in the bedroom mirror. He had his tracksuit bottoms on, an Aran shawl-neck sweater tucked in and a towel over his shoulders. The glamour of his look was completed by his gold chain and the sunglasses. He smoothed down his thick moustache and squirted a few more drops of relaxer on to his perm. Badd Zaf, he called himself. 'Just like Jackie Shroff.' That was who he was trying to look like, some Bollywood bad guy. To complete the image, he'd recently taken up smoking.

Zaf's two young nephews worshipped him. They followed

him about, one at each elbow, looking into his face and attempting to capture the essence of his cool. At odd moments Paul had seen them repeating something their heroic uncle had just said, the phrases sounding daft coming from their lips. 'Hamid's nose got broke bad ways!' or 'I tell you them's serious vibes, big time!' Or they'd bob and spin, muttering things like 'Nuff Respec'! Wha 'appen, spar?'

It always cracked Paul up to see his Asian friends acting black. Badd Zaf always made him laugh anyway. There he was polishing up his gangsta image and yet as soon as Paul told him that the neighbours had started dismantling stolen cars, he was all for going to the police.

'You're joking, aren't you? We can't inform on them.'

'But those are *gora* man. White honkies, man, *blud claat*. They're not like you and me.'

'What difference does that make?'

'The difference is they're not in the ghetto, man.'

'What're you on about? The red-haired bloke lives in that house. Well, his wife does and he's there now and again.'

Zaf turned, looking meaningfully over the top of his shades, and adopted his irritating movie star voice. 'The ghetto is a skin thing, spar, not a place.'

'Rubbish!'

'No way, man. They don't live under the same rules as us. What if it was a black operation, huh? The Feds would have closed it down by now.'

'They never shut down your mountain bike racket.'

Zaf dismissed the suggestion with a theatrical wave of his hand. 'Bikes is bikes – we're talking *cars* here, man, and lots of them.'

'I thought you said you shifted nearly forty bikes?'

'Forty-five, actually. I shifted forty-five in three months. Sweet sweet days. Shame the university caught on so soon. But those were two wheels, Rasta, not four. How many have gone through there so far? Five in three weeks?' Zaf fiddled with the calculator on his watch, prodding at the tiny buttons with a match. 'That's eighty-six point six six six per year if they keep up the same pace.' The match became a toothpick. 'They're not being careful, man. It doesn't make good business sense. They deserve to be shopped.'

'Well there's no way *I'm* going to shop them,' said Paul, calling his friend's bluff. '*You* can if you want but for me they're just making a living like everyone else.'

Badd Zaf back-pedalled fast at the challenge. 'I'm not saying I'm going to,' he said. 'I'm just saying it's within your rights if you do.'

'Well, I'm not going to,' said Paul, again.

Nevertheless, when, after car number six, the months went by and the yard remained empty, he was relieved. Then one day – it was spring by then – number seven arrived and changed everything. Number seven was different, a spotless white Capri, the type of car that had become rare and was driven for the most part by older men with low insurance premiums and golf clubs on the back seat. Except that this Capri looked special. Not over-the-top customized but somehow slightly wider, slightly lower. The two bubbles on the bonnet suggested an unusually large engine. It was a mystery. Paul puzzled over his catalogues at home but found nothing that corresponded. The early removal of the plates added to his difficulties.

It was immaculate. Between the April showers its bodywork glistened like a well-polished jewel. As he watched it seemed to glow, inviolate, indignant at being cooped up in such mean surroundings. That didn't last long. It soon surrendered to the man with the heavy jaw and tree-trunk neck and the oily little weasel busy with his wrench. Over the next two days, like time-lapse photography, the stages of its decay sped by. Lights, bonnet, doors, interior, all disappeared. The replacement of the wheels with a battered old set habitually used for each car's final journey dispelled any remaining aura. Then, suddenly, the space where it had been sitting was empty once more – except for a wheel brace and a complicated and unrecognizable engine part, like an archaeological relic. The ringers had become very practised by that time.

The demise of the Capri pushed Paul's tolerance to its limit and beyond. His father had bought a similar car a few years before and he had watched and 'helped' him do it up to sell on. A Capri had a special feel, Paul knew that. It wasn't one of the over-priced, over-powered sports models with no handling, as insubstantial as a paper bag with a V6. His dad had let him drive the car over by the derelict works on Sundays. He knew how Capris pulled heavily, like a tank; how they cut through the air like a slab of solid metal. He knew how they cornered with the grace of a full metric tonne. He had felt the tyre-tread part against the tarmac when cornering; he had fed the steering wheel between his palms. This car was different. He hadn't cared about any of the others but this was a real car in the old style. Like Zaf's uncle's, but royal with it. It was a car that transcended questions of race or loyalty to social class, even hatred of the police and the judicial process. After all, thought Paul, you have to value something in this life, you have to have a passion for something. His mother had told him that, and he knew that belief would take him far, even though he sometimes thought it separated him from his mates at school and some of those in the park. He'd watched the ringers, how they took something whole and trashed it. He'd found it hard to see them do that to this car. He had to let the police know. Still he hesitated, feeling unable to tell Zaf about his attachment. But when it finally disappeared like all the others, he walked round to sound out Zaf on the subject.

'There's a white Capri been dumped out the back,' Zaf said excitedly as soon as Paul appeared. A quick reconnoitre established that it was the same one. It was a sorry sight. Languishing – number seven – in the alleyway behind Zaf's row of terraces. The alley was strewn with rubbish. A rat – victim of the council's Pest Control Unit – lay dead on the kerb. Squat on its raised axles, its inside a mess of wire and exposed steel, the wreck didn't look out of place. You couldn't have guessed that it was – had been – a Ford Capri. Only the shape might have given it away, the low long body and aerodynamic cab, the slope of the windscreen perhaps. Now it was stripped of just about everything saleable, just a husk. Paul stood next to it, silent, awestruck by how the mighty had been brought low. He lifted one hand and ran it along the mute, gleaming, curved steel of the roof.

'It's come from those ringers two doors down from me. I see they took the spoiler,' said Paul, running his fingers over the twisted rivet stubs that had attached it to the boot.

'Nah,' said Zaf. 'The two Pathan lads from next door but one had that.'

'Eh?'

Zaf eyed the carcass. 'Yeah, I came out here and there was a group of people crowded round. Next door said it had just been dumped. He saw the blokes who did it. I asked him if he'd called the police and he said "Not yet" so I said "Good, I just want the battery." Then another bloke said he wanted the wipers and someone else the front grille. It only took us about twenty minutes.'

Jackals, thought Paul. Like jackals round carrion. It was as though the whole neighbourhood was involved. Nevertheless, later, the arrival of the owner crystallized Paul's determination to act and finish the ringers for good. Here was a man, probably retired, who obviously had money, enough money to afford a jeep and wear stylish clothes, but despite his flashy appearance, his age and colour of skin, when he spoke Paul could sense that they shared something, that passion; that insistence on value. Here was another connoisseur, someone who understood. They were the same in that.

Perhaps it was his anger (or was it fear of them?), but the man showed little interest in what Paul had to say. He began by accusing the crowd of young men and then slagged off the whole neighbourhood. Paul knew it would be best to speak with him alone. He was probably intimidated by them, that was all. Responsibility for the loss of the car weighed Paul down. Why hadn't he acted sooner? Beyond the boundaries of race and age, Paul saw that this was a wrong he was able to put right. If he was in the old man's place he would have felt gutted. But he could make amends.

Thinking his course of action through when the others had gone, Paul realized he couldn't talk to the owner there and then. What, risk being led to point the finger at a neighbour and incur the retribution of Tree-neck? No, the information would have to be given to the police by phone. An anonymous tip-off. If he was quick, most of the parts could be retrieved. He felt a warmth inside as his plan took shape, a warmth not dampened by the Dirty Harry manner of a policeman who arrived on the scene a few minutes later. It would be like the hand of fate. He could help restore the old man's happiness. The policeman had that teacherish, you-do-as-you're-told attitude about him now, but Paul took no notice. Seeing the despair etched on to the tanned face of the owner and imagining joy there when the ringers were caught and the parts retrieved, Paul couldn't help smiling.

Like a child. Like a five-year-old boy blubbing. Sidney Davis looked at himself in the mirror above the sink. He looked at his thinning grey hair ('silver' Margaret liked to call it); at the ridged frown grooves on his expanding brown forehead almost as though someone had drawn a comb across the flesh. Then back at his eyes. It was no good. They were red rimmed and Margaret would guess. He wondered for a moment how it was that emotion – crying, he really meant – was somehow so much easier, the older he got. Cry baby. They'd used to call him that at school, what? It must be more than fifty years ago now. Cry baby, crying over his lost toy. Only what he had lost, or rather what had been stolen from him was much, much more than a toy.

The phone call had come at half past one, its plaintive chirrup cutting through the *Archers* theme as Margaret rinsed the last few dishes after lunch. Of course, Sidney answered it at once and she tensed and listened, wondering how bad the news would be. She could hear her husband's voice, almost toneless, posing question after question into the mouthpiece. It was an effort for him to conceal his worry. He had spent two hours in the downstairs cloakroom or in the hallway, sitting on the stool by the teak telephone table, leafing through one of his back issues of *Classic Car*, waiting for the blessed telephone to ring. He was like – she trembled slightly at the thought – an anxious parent waiting for news about a missing loved one. As she suspected, he had been crying. That thought stifled her anger, an anger that was often her main emotion when she dwelt on how long he spent in the garage with his fellow enthusiasts. Enthusiasts! They were nothing more than boys to her way of thinking. Meanwhile, she was left alone in their childless, empty house.

However, it no longer irritated her. It was his character, who he was. She wiped a few scattered crumbs off the kitchen table and into her cupped hand. From there she transferred them carefully on to the breadboard; the birds would enjoy them. Only that naughty tabby from two doors along had been loitering in the garden again. Pippa she was called and she was the chief suspect for the decline and decease of a rather choice fromontia Margaret had acquired from Webbs at Wychbold the summer before. Pippa's poisonous pee. She would have to get Sidney to devise a way of keeping the cat away from her plants. She blenched as she heard him crunch the receiver back into its cradle and then immediately open the front door and close it behind him. Putting the cloth down beside the sink, she hurried out after him.

He was already behind the wheel of the jeep and could barely bring himself to look at her. 'Sidney, darling? It's been found then?'

'Yes.'

'Where?'

He hesitated. 'Of all places, they've found it in Sparkbrook. Not far from where I grew up.'

'Sparkbrook? But that's *miles* away. How horrible! Is it badly damaged?'

'They couldn't give me any details.' Sidney sighed heavily, his face looking suddenly haggard. Margaret reached forward tentatively to touch his hand, half knowing it would do no good. He withdrew it to turn the key in the ignition. 'It's best I get over there as quickly as I can.'

She watched the car glide past the succession of neatly manicured lawns and disappear out of the close.

With a crunch of splintered bottle glass the open-top jeep rounded the corner of the alleyway from the street. It pulled up sharply ten yards from a group of youths clustered about the remains of the Capri. Sidney climbed carefully out. He ignored them as he approached, trying hard to shrug off the sense of vulnerability that enveloped him along with the squalor of the streets, that once – before the brown tide had drowned them – he had called his own. It was worse than he could ever have imagined. The group watched fascinated as, warding off a sudden dizziness, he walked round his car, muttering to himself.

'Is it yours, mate?' One of them, taller than the rest, a half-caste boy (the others were Asians: Pakistanis, Sidney supposed) spoke up.

Mate? There was insolence in the boy's manner. Distraught, Sidney focused his attention for a second, took in the speaker's expression and appearance. Everything about him suggested a set of values different from his own. And not just the boy's but those of his parents too. Or more likely, his *parent*. He had heard the story many times: a shiftless coal-black father who'd preyed on some easily fooled supermarket check-out girl. When it fell apart she was left with a baby. From there, decline, sedmentation. It wasn't her fault. But it did condense down to this: mixed-up offspring with an inability to recognize and respect seniority; children handicapped by the narrow life of these streets, unable to make judgements of people from elsewhere.

'Mate?'

'She was mine, yes.' He allowed a strong note of sarcasm to colour his response.

'When was it stolen?'

Sidney hated the whole situation. Wouldn't he be better off getting back in his jeep and driving off, now that he'd found the Capri? There was indignity in having his distress exposed to this group of scruffy youths. As he pivoted away his shoes crunched on fragments of quarter-light glass (more thievery, more mindless destruction) and he stopped himself. He couldn't leave. The ruin of his most prized possession sat in front of him. What more might happen to it if he left it, even for a few minutes?

He spoke low and lumpily, almost to himself. 'She disappeared barely forty-eight hours ago. The people who stole her were obviously professionals. They got past a crook-lock, a Longarm and an immobilizer under the bonnet. Somehow they managed it. What can you do to stop people like that?' His eyes were glazed under the effort of trying to comprehend what he saw. Without warning, he sank heavily down on to the kerb and sat, despite his clothes and tan, reduced to a sad old man. 'I don't believe it, I can't believe anyone would do a thing like this.' He didn't see the tall boy move one cautious step towards him. Mindful of his audience once more, he got stiffly back to his feet and now wore his misfortune stonily on his face, storing it away for a time and place more private.

'Where was it stolen from?' The tall youth spoke again, his head tilting on his shoulders in what Sidney took to be a parody of sympathy.

'From outside my house in Bromsgrove.'

One of the Asians – the one wearing dark glasses although the alley lay in shadow – spoke up. 'I thought I seen it round here before.' When he spoke, he opened and spread his hands with weighty emphasis. The others deferred to him and he seemed to savour that power like a junior Godfather.

The owner responded coldly, a prick of malice seeking to burst the boy's bubble of authority. 'Round here? Don't be ridiculous. For your information, there aren't any other cars quite like this one.' He regretted the outburst immediately. Not because he saw the boy flinch at his contempt but because slackening the leash on his emotions now meant he had to dig his heels in to prevent himself being dragged down a slippery slope. The group of boys evidently sensed it too, picking out the ripples of anguish he kept just below the surface of his voice. 'No, I can state for a fact that you've never seen a car like this before because I've been the sole owner ever since it was driven out of the works at Dagenham.

I only take her for a spin once a year and I don't make a habit of driving around *this* area of the city.' He stood looking into the space once covered by a bonnet. There was no engine there now. He shifted away to the far side of the car, scratching his head. 'I'd better get in touch with my insurance people.'

The tall boy, who was probably the leader, stepped forward. 'It's a Capri, isn't it?'

Sidney nodded but there was disapproval and suspicion in his look. 'None of you know anything about it, I suppose?' He felt stupid as soon as he'd asked it. If present, the guilty party would scoff at such a naïve question. He looked at each face. Wasn't there a note of subdued glee in their questions? He tensed. Surely he was asking for trouble, coming alone into this area. He had been so anxious to get his car back, to see that it was still in one piece but once he entered the labyrinth of terraced streets, his keenness had subsided into a daze. Had he really grown up here? Brunswick, Chesterton, Newton: the street names in the *A–Z* had given no clue that where the sorry, white shell of the car had been ditched had mutated grotesquely into an alien, poverty-stricken slum quarter. It was a world in which he did not belong, in which he felt his natural authority shorn away. Here his age, his class carried no weight.

'We live here,' said the leader with a sort of angry defiance as if he'd been reading the owner's thoughts. 'We're not likely to do this and dump it on our own doorstep, are we?'

'I don't know. *Aren't* you?' He kicked at the unassemblable jigsaw of quarter-light glass at his feet. 'Look around you. Areas like this breed this kind of crime.' However, even as he said it a tongue of alarm started to hammer in the bell of his chest: he was alone in the middle of a gang of what his neighbour Ron would call 'coloured yobs' in a seedy rat-infested alleyway. He needed to be careful. His district of neat lawns and tidy houses had been no preparation for anything he might encounter here. He had last felt like this the night he drove home from Sandra and Freddy's barbecue the summer before and the blue and white light of a police car froze his hands solid to his steering wheel when it overtook. He had been so sure they were going to pull him over, but they'd taken a sharp right and screeched off past a rhododendron bush. He wondered now if he was going to be sick. 'After all, she didn't get far without wheels and in that state, did she?' His control slackened again. 'I can't believe it. I had her resprayed only last month. What they've done is . . . The appalling thing is whoever did it probably didn't even know what they were destroying.'

A rumble and clatter swelling from behind the last terraced house caught the attention of the group and their solemnity faltered. Two small boys charged into the alleyway. One was pushing the other along on a broken skateboard. They stopped when they saw the scene in front of them, stood and gawped at their reflections in the wing of the old man's jeep, then moved quickly to join the others, their eyes still wide.

Sidney turned his face away for a second. He couldn't show weakness. He had to bury his fear. But it was a struggle to keep the rawness out of his voice. 'As far as I'm concerned you lot are all involved in this. Anyone can tell just by looking at you.' He let that sink in. There were no denials, so he built on it. 'I don't know what you're standing around for anyway. You better make yourself scarce before the police come back because, believe me, I'm going to call them. Now get lost, go on!'

The Asian boy looked over the rims of his sunglasses. 'OK, boss, keep your hair on.' The two little boys with the skateboard – perhaps they were his younger brothers – watched him and started imitating him as soon as he'd finished speaking. 'Cut it out, you two.' He cuffed one of them.

'You'd better watch your step – all of you. I've got a good memory for faces.' Sidney stopped his hand involuntarily toying with his keys, suddenly becoming aware that their nervy jingle undermined the confidence of his words. To his relief, the gang began to disperse. A game of football had started up in the park opposite the row of houses. Excited shouts could be heard and the thud of the ball as it was kicked high in the evening air. The sounds drew the gang like a magnet. Only the tall one seemed reluctant to leave.

Sidney returned to his jeep and began dialling a number on the mobile phone he had pulled from a holster at his hip as the group left the alley. He would call the police anyway. They had said the car was drivable. It was outrageous. Like saying, 'You sort it out. We can't be bothered.' He spoke briefly, curtly to the officer on duty and told him the situation.

The tall boy with the leather jacket still stood there, his hands in his pockets, gazing at the wreck. 'I'll catch up with you,' he called to the retreating figures and waited expectantly.

Next, Sidney called his mechanic. Blast – the number was engaged. He felt empty. This alley, so unlike the quiet, sun-filled cul-de-sacs where he lived, had sucked out his will, just as it had sucked his treasured possession in and left a ruin. The network of streets was a web and his car had been trapped like a glittering beetle. He'd come only to retrieve its empty carapace, its sucked dry shell. And where had its value – all the years of care and money he had expended on it – gone? Lost; it was a debasement that could yield no comparable return. The paint on the doors and window-frames of these streets weren't glowing a rejuvenated white because of it, they were still peeling and flaky. A crisp packet twirled a mocking scratchy pirouette in the gutter in front of him as though celebrating his loss. Now he looked around himself in horror, sensing the monstrous Shelob impulse that had stripped his car might at the next moment make him its victim too. Waves of despair and anger again gave way to a commotion of fear. Was he going to be mugged as well, to top it all? He climbed gingerly out of the jeep. 'Are you still here?'

The boy had obviously not finished gloating. 'I wanted to tell you that I'm sorry about what's happened.'

'Sorry? You're sorry. Oh. And is there anything else? Have you got anything *useful* you want to tell me? Like who's responsible for this . . . this mess?'

A surprised look came over the boy's features.

'Well?'

'I just want to say that I sympathize,' stammered the youth.

Sidney could barely keep his temper under control. 'Do you think that makes any difference to me? Your sympathy? Your sympathy isn't going to bring my car back, is it? You're hardly likely to understand that that car was worth more than you've ever seen. An amount people of your sort dream about.' There was raw emotion in his voice now, anger and hurt. He didn't let up. Each sentence of the tirade hammered his fury home. 'Not that this is just about money because if it was I'd pay to have it fixed immediately. The fact is, the parts you and your neighbourhood have stolen are unobtainable. There *are* not spares because the car was unique. She was a collector's item. Fifteen years old, a prototype of a series that was a development of the SR 3.5 injection. Ford abandoned the project and I drove away a piece of motoring history. It's going to take me years to have the parts made and have her rebuilt. So you can save your sympathy. Now, was there anything *else*?'

Shrinking beneath the shower of contempt, the youth frowned and looked him in the eye. 'Nothing else.' He turned away and started walking in the direction of the football game but stopped at the sound of another vehicle approaching.

Experiencing an intensity of relief that bordered on physical pleasure, Sidney watched a police car turn into the alleyway. Rescue. Here at last was someone who could reassert the proper order of things.

'Right then. Is this your car, sir?' The policeman was blond and brusque.

'That's right, officer.'

The effect on the youth of the panda car's arrival had been startling. He'd somehow retreated from the circle created by the wreck and its owner. So he *had* been about to do something, had been left alone by the others, the better, the more discreetly to achieve it. What hurt Sidney further was how the policeman, accustomed to leering bystanders perhaps, seemed not to see him. Sidney's powerless frustration boiled up again. Was he supposed to join in this charade? To say nothing, pretend nothing was amiss? He could already imagine his enemy's knowing smirk as he offered mock 'sympathy' from the sidelines. And was he supposed to surrender to it, paralysed like just another item of prey? He would *not*. He just *wouldn't*.

'This boy, with a number of others, was looking over the car when I arrived. I suspect he knows something.' Try as he might, Sidney wasn't able to keep the emotion out of his voice.

The policeman was beside the car now. The look he gave it was strange. It seemed to register surprise, disbelief, then a grim elation. He turned on the youth's slinking form. 'You! Come over here. Now!' Sidney's blood fizzed at the commanding tone.

The boy stopped in his sloping tracks but did not turn, as if he had half heard or only half understood the order.

'I *said* come here.' Legs slightly apart, the neb of his cap tilted menacingly down like a tank's turret twisting to take aim, the policeman was in complete control.

The absurd, clumpy trainers scuffed unwillingly across the tarmac in obedience. The eyes held fast to the ground as if to lose hold would mean a long, dangerous fall. The rounded shoulders, not yet a man's, quaked as the boy stood in front of Sidney and the policeman.

The uniformed voice barked, '*Do* you know anything about this? *Do* you?'

Headshake. Perhaps it was better left there – his subsiding anger told Sidney that order had been restored, that was enough. Then the boy looked up. His wide eyes were directed not at the policeman but at Sidney and, suddenly, he smiled.

The smile made Sidney feel uneasy. Perhaps he had been over-hasty in his judgement of the boy. He was about to say so, to get the officer to drop it, but the first rush of his words was severed by an adroit step forward that coincided precisely with a swiftly punched out fist. It happened too quickly, with not a flicker of emotion showing on the policeman's face. An instant later, the boy was doubled up on the tarmac, gulping at the air with a braying sound.

In a reasonable voice, the policeman spoke again. 'Then it would be best if you went about your business.' The boy attempted to stand up, then staggered off, unstrung and uncoordinated like a tangled marionette, pausing against the fence for breath. 'Go on. Fuck off out of it,' the policeman's voice hissed after him.

It was unnerving how the officer's tone changed when he turned and gave Sidney his full attention. 'Now, sir, are you going to organize to have it towed home? I need to get a few details down.'

Five minutes later and he was gone. Sidney, still shaken, was back on the phone giving the location of the wreck to his mechanic. 'Gus? I've found it . . . No, it's standing in front of me . . . I can barely believe it . . . what's left of it. It's been stripped but I think we can do something. I want you to get the truck down here immediately. You'll have to bring a set of wheels . . . I can't say, we'll have to get it back and look it over . . . In an alleyway off Rushton Road, Sparkbrook. I'll see you back at the garage in half an hour. We'll look her over then.'

The game was well underway when Paul got there. The same faces from the alleyway were now flushed with pleasure. They surged and jostled in pursuit of the ball, the old white man and his troubles forgotten. Rather than joining in, Paul sat down on a bench at the edge of the tarmac pitch to watch Badd Zaf in his shades dazzling the younger ones with his skills. The two nephews, Arif and Asif, were over by the swings, preparing to skateboard down the slide. Paul sat, pensive.

The frenzy of the football game lapsed for a few minutes while the ball was retrieved from the rooftop of a nearby carpet warehouse. Badd Zaf approached, a fresh cigarette dangling from his lips. 'What did the Babylon say?'

'Nothing important.'

'Has the tow truck turned up yet?'

Paul shook his head. 'Can I borrow your lighter?'

Zaf started in mock surprise. 'Since when have you been smoking? You shouldn't – you'll end up with a habit like Badd Zaf's. Here you go.' He tossed him his Zippo. 'You know, maybe we should have told the old man who did it.'

Slipping the lighter into his pocket, Paul scowled. He was thinking of the locals clustered round the Capri, picking it clean of its remaining morsels. He'd been wrong. They weren't like jackals around carrion, no. They were more like coastal villagers in the past gathering the storm-spoils of the latest wreck from the beach.'Told him? You heard what he said. We're all guilty in his eyes. Just living here makes us guilty.'

They both looked up as the jeep rounded the corner and accelerated away. The owner had apparently got tired of waiting. 'Back in a minute,' said Paul.

Badd Zaf stopped him. 'You heard what he said, he's got a good memory for faces.'

Paul shrugged off the warning hand. 'Nah, we're ghetto. This is what he expects.' A crease of pain momentarily slanted the line of his mouth. 'We all look the same to him, anyway.' And then, as an afterthought, he added over his shoulder, 'Call it a skin thing.'

By the time the tow truck arrived ten minutes later, the football match was underway again. There was an eerie light in the sky now, a pinkish glow that was not caused solely by the setting sun. From behind the terrace of houses a fire flickered, sending up slick coils of black smoke into the hot evening sky.

The Blue Bridge

Gul Davis

She touches me softly. 'Meet me under the arches of the Blue Bridge.' Her tongue circles the inner of my ear, leaving a layer of saliva. A hand on either cheek, she lowers her body against my face, breasts brushing my nose. Kissing my lips, she lets go and runs naked down the grey pebble-grind beach, wading against the waves until her long blond hair floats, a tangled path behind her as she swims. I watch, till she's out of sight. Maybe drowned; maybe, like she says, beneath the sea in a city that exists down there. Her hands were cold as ocean waters in winter; she smelled of sea-weed. Lying down on the beach, I buckle into my coat and go to sleep.

The tide wakes me, dampness clawing through denim and canvas, water washing against my fingers mirroring their shape as it seeps away. My nose is filled with the smell of rotting weed and salt, my shoe has half sunk into the wet sand, the roar of waves is loud in my ears. I open my eyes, they are covered with silt; my whole body is covered in white silt. Must have looked like a lump of raised sand from a distance last night. Maybe nobody realized I was a man lying there, perhaps they thought I was just part of the beach.

Standing up, I don't bother to brush the sand off me. I walk knee-deep into the green choppy waters and wash my face in the cold. Squelching out of the water in my Doc Martens. Pebbles grumble, rattling under my soles. Beach: the border between land and sea. Climbing over the wall, I step on to the pavement and stare at the dead shops on the other side of the road, still closed.

Gower Street: silent, no cars rolling, no people, shop-fronts declaring 'closed' on their doors. Steel shutters drawn. My feet leave prints of my shoes on the paving slabs. I run my finger down the canvas. I look at the sand collected on my index finger. I run a line down, a line across; a crucifix marked on the sleeve. I turn down Stanley Road; parked cars on either side leave only a small space between them. Climbing the stairs of number seven, I bang my fist on a sky blue door. 'Jackie!' I bang the door again.

The door wedges open. 'It's fucking five in the morning, Will! What have you been doing?'

'Sorry, Sis.' Pushing my way in, I slip my boots off. My blue socks are soaking wet.

'Quiet, you'll wake Sam. He's just gone back to sleep.'

'Is he still feeding like there's no tomorrow?'

Sis glances down at her swollen chest, at the two damp patches on her nightie. 'Yeah. I'm going back to bed.'

Sleep isn't an easy place for me. I sit and watch the TV drift from night-time telly to early morning news. I push myself from the sofa, pull off my jacket, jeans, my jumper, T-shirt, treading off my socks. I leave them in a heap on the living-room floor.

The shower bites. Rolling, spitting, washing off dirt and sleep. Tiredness, the trek from the hostel in Birmingham.

Police might put the warrant out today, or tomorrow, depends when they hear. Mr Solemn will have told them that I haven't turned up for work. I rub the soap into a lather about my body, it feels good. Good to stretch and clean, to scrub, to let the warmth eat, gently ease the harsh sea cold. To see my feet turn from blue to pink, my hands from white and strained. Loneliness. I can feel it in each isolated drop that hits me, spat from the shower head. I cannot rub it off with the water as I dry myself. I wander naked round Sis's flat, look at her and the baby huddled together in the double bed. The cot; barren and alone. It's good to hear, see them sleep, their gentle breath . . .

The news is still ranting. I press my face on the window pane and watch the street wake. Condensation stifles my view. I mark a crucifix with my finger, watch it fade as my breath cools. I need to go out; see if I can find her.

The Doc Martens hurt. I take them off and leave them lop-sided on the pebble beach. The sea, retreated, leaves a damp clay-coloured dune. In the distance I see her walking out of the faraway water. Her long golden hair wet, matted, round her shoulders; her skin as she comes close covered in goose pimples.

She crouches down and hugs me. Into her naked flesh I cry. I feel so alone. My fingers dig into her skin, the heat from my tears blurring my vision. A finger runs against my eye, catches a tear. She places the tear in her mouth.

'Will, why are you so sad?' Her face moves close, her blue eyes stare into mine. Clutching her, I can't breathe for the tears choking my chest as they spill in stuttered sobs. Straddling her legs either side of me, in the cutting wind, we sit on the bare beach far from shore.

'Leave,' she says, drawing away. 'Leave, with me.' Standing, she pulls me from the beach, leading me towards the sea. Its waters return up the barren sandbanks. My bare feet sink into the silt. We step into the waves as they lap around us. She looks at me, smiles. Taking my other hand, she draws me, walking backwards into the waves, waist deep.

'Bessy!' A voice from behind us. She looks up. Her face grows old. I turn. A man calls from the shore. I feel her let go, she is gone.

'See you've met our Bess.' He crouches down in the pebbles, chewing, spits pale phlegm on to the stones. His face is beaten to a worn scorched leather, his blue eyes burn bright from their sockets . . .

I squat next to him. 'She is beautiful.'

'That she is, but down in her coffin she is as rotten and putrid as any other corpse, if there is any flesh left after all these years.'

'I thought she was a dream.' I angle my thumb in my mouth and chew my thumbnail, bitten to the quick.

The man flicks to a stand, grabs my chin, thumb and finger digging into my face. 'She's real!' He spits to his left, his gaze buries itself in my eyes. Pale and blue and scared. 'She's the phantom of Bessy Jones.'

'Get the fuck off me.' I pull free from his hand, clench my fist tight. 'Don't fucking grab me!' I step back, keeping my gaze locked with his. Gnarled and lean, he turns away.

'She'll lead you to your death, boy.' He kicks pebbles my way with his heel. 'She'll drown you.' His tall figure angles, walks slowly towards the wall bordering the road.

The stench of seaweed. A dead smell. Phantom Bessy Jones. I grimace, looking out across the water, where waist deep I had been walking against the waves, led by a naked girl who disappeared . . . Am I seeing things? Going mad again? The cold, clammy wet denim of my jeans, crusted with the salt of yesterday. Water sinks through, turning my thighs blue and goose-pimpled. I place my palm on my wet trousers, spread my hand, star shaped. The touch of her breast against my face . . . What had I been doing wading in the water? Walking towards the road I cast a gaze over the ocean.

I stay away from the sea. It makes me feel cold, the smell of rotting seaweed stays in my nostrils as if something dead is lodged; following me. There had been no warmth in her fingertips, no warmth in her palms as she touched.

Dusk sets. The lights burn in shop-fronts. I make my way down Gower Street looking at the people with their carrier bags full, skulking to their cars.

Cars pack either side of Stanley Road, crook-locked and alarmed. A brown Sierra double parked in front of Sis's flat. Sis opens the front door, Sam cuddled in her arms, nuzzling under her armpit. She mouths at me. I turn on my heels and run.

Police burst from around her. The Sierra reverses, clipping my side.

'William Tucker. Stop. This is the police!' I feel a hand grasp my elbow and slip. I stride long, hard, pushing myself forward, Gower Street, the shops. I push past a fat man drawing his little girl towards him. The policeman knocks straight into them, they tangle, a hard thump on the pavement. The little girl screams. Can hear more feet pounding after me.

The Blue Bridge over the estuary curves upward in front of me, my breath wheezes from my chest, a long choked gasp. Sweat trickles down my face, sticking shirt to skin. Pounding footsteps: they're still there! I can't breathe. The Sierra, driving over from the other side of the bridge, brakes and swerves, blocking the pavement and half the road. Doors smack open. Policemen climb out. I throw myself at the railing, looking down at the water as hands grapple, twisting my arms, cuffing me. I can feel the metal rings bite as they lock.

I stare at her as they manhandle me.

Bessy has come to drown me. The police to lock me away.

Tears stream. 'Stop blabbering.' The policeman's tone is coarse.

'Jump, Will. Come to me.' Her voice inside my head sounds like the murmur of water.

'So you can bloody drown me!' I cry.

'Who are you talking to?' The policeman shouts, grabs my chin, turns my face.

'Trust me, Will,' she whispers. 'For once in your life, trust!' The policeman slaps me hard. I push myself over the railings. Falling, arms cuffed behind my back. Smack, the water slaps. Bessy grabs my feet, pulling me under. I breathe in, the sea water chokes, coughing and spluttering, more sea water retches in my chest. Bessy's grip is firm, her hands grabbed tightly around my ankles. She pulls me under. I scream. Bubbles burst around me, silver marbles popping. Each a cry for help, exhausted by the time they disappear. Through the murkiness I look down at Bessy, dragging me further under, hands tight like vices as she smiles at me. She opens her mouth.

I can hear the roll of waves. Wet clammy sand. Seaweed slides between my fingers.

'Are you all right, son?' A bony hand shakes me.

Squinting through eyes red-raw and stinging, a blurred face, small and old, huddles over me. White hair folded in the wrap of her shawl.

'Bessy?'

She shakes her head. 'No, I'm not Bessy. Bessy died long ago. She was my daughter when she was alive. Come now, it's cold and the tide is drawing in.'

I choke, vomit salt water.

'You're the second one this year, the second one I've found half drowned.' A coarse, creaking chuckle. 'You're a lucky man, son. She cares about you, to leave you here. Had I not known to come . . . well, let's just say few others are aware of this cove.'

Tears run. Placing a hand behind the back of my neck, the old woman lifts my head. 'You have a sister? Go to her. Bessy says you're in need. Come, son, you'll catch your death out here.'

Dedicated to Liane Aukin and Carole Satyamurti

Grey

Mark Newton

Awake again to the taste of yesterday and furniture, the television set in the corner still pouring black and white confusion into the room. The phone woke me up. It was beeping at me like *Road Runner*. Shut up, I said, but it wasn't listening; either that or it didn't hear. I spoke quite quietly because Phil takes the piss when he catches me speaking to machines.

I think something might be crawling in my mouth. On my forehead there's a beam of light like the red dot sighting on a sniper rifle, the kind you get in movies. The red dot tells me it's morning, otherwise I wouldn't know. My watch stopped a long time ago. It drowned in piss and yoghurt on the floor. Outside, colour has surrendered. The grey streets meet the grey buildings meet the grey sky and the monochrome mess means no one can distinguish the floor from the firmament. Well, that's what it was like last time I looked, anyway. I haven't been out there in a while. Here inside, four bars of that fanatical daylight struggle to beat the maze of walls and push their way in. I wish they wouldn't. There are no windows here. There is a hole in the door where a window used to be. It had been reinforced with wire and

Seth had seen it as a challenge to his manhood when he was more coked up than usual. He stood there for quarter of an hour battering it with an ironing board until it gave in. I cheered him on then. I was probably drunk. The hole only faces another room, though, not the grey, and the light has to push its way past the glass in the kitchen – that we ceded to the rats – before it can even peer through the hole into the lounge.

There is definitely something in my mouth, and I think there's something in my hair too. Maybe it's because I'm at one with the animals. I was the one who first offered the rats Coco Pops. The light, quartered by the window-frame in the kitchen, forms the shadow of a cross in the air. Seth likes to think it's some kind of blessing; the Good Lord. That's one of the reasons I resent it. Seth likes to think all kinds of things. He thinks Anne Frank's diary is a fraud. He says they carbon-dated it and found it was written in the fifties. Too many ideas and all of them stupid. That's what got us in this mess in the first place. I always say 'like the Turin Shroud' and he stares through me like I was made out of tracing paper.

I cough, and along with the normal blood, tar and mucus there's a dead ant. At least it's not a beetle. I really need a drink. My messy eyes can only see empty bottles. Oh fuck, and Sunkist cans. Nobody drinks Sunkist. It's bad for your teeth. I must have passed out early last night. I force myself to open my eyes fully. I don't like doing that sober. At least all the furniture is still here this time. Seth got about forty quid's worth of dust off Ralph for the last lot. Only Ralph brings round Sunkist cans. He says they're the best kind, something to do with the thickness of the aluminium. I used to think his name was Alf. I thought the name Alf was funny. I've got a bad sense of humour. Before I'd seen his face I'd had visions of a hairy alien and that fat guy from *Home and*

Away merged together. Ralph didn't look like that. The TV is still producing interference. I look for the remote for the video. I need a war to watch.

A guy has stepped into the room. The mud of my head can still tell it's Phil. No one else looks so normal. He wears the uniform of youth: blue jeans, checked shirt, black jeans, Ralph Lauren shirt, one or the other. Hair shaved, ordinary. He looks around, knowing what to expect, sighs, and lights a cigarette.

'Can you crash us one of those?'

Phil's shoulder jumps. I'm not sure whether it's out of surprise or if he's just started twitching again. 'Yeah, sure.'

I light it and begin to fill my mouth with the old and new stains of today. An ant crawls from my teeth on to the filter and then decides to jump for it.

'You look like a fuckin' corpse.'

'No I don't. I look like River Phoenix,' I say. I do. I bought a jacket just like the one he wore in *My Own Private Idaho*. I have to admit that my skin is a little whiter these days, my eyes a little darker. And I haven't eaten anything except Yop for a couple of weeks. But I do look like River Phoenix. Phil is smirking.

'Can you see the remote anywhere?' I ask.

'Yeah, it's over there by the bin.' Phil points.

'Which bit?'

The whole room is a bin; it just happens to start with a plastic container in the corner. Everyone threw their stuff at it and once it got covered by a pizza box or something it just kept spilling over, like an octopus in a goldfish bowl. The floor, lino half melted by cigarette ends, looks like sludge-flavoured bubble-wrap. When Seth was really fucked he used to burst the pustules with his thumbs. He thought it was therapeutic. And he would spit on it when he got up in the evening. No one complained. You couldn't really tell.

Only Phil noticed when he pissed on it. That's when I lost time. It didn't seem worth saving once I found out what happened to it. Now I can't tell the minutes from the days, it all just blurs into one. That's what got us into this mess in the first place.

You can barely see the floor anyway, covered with half-eaten food, balti dishes, old newspapers, fag boxes, Cellophane, smashed pint glasses, stale beer, a variety of plastic and glass bottles, a litter of receipts from every delivery store – a life of convenience. There's a solitary KFC box. That's worse than the Sunkist cans. Nobody eats KFC. They don't deliver. It doesn't look dangerous, but these things just sneak up on you. You can never tell what's going to be important. When Ralph brought the box round I presumed he was eating chicken. It's what you'd think, isn't it? He didn't open it for a while. I figured his food would be getting cold, and I didn't want him using our microwave because last time Phil cooked in the kitchen he got gastro-enteritis. He shitted green for a week. It was funny when it happened to him. It wouldn't be funny if it happened to Ralph. Anyway, the box remained firmly shut until he went upstairs with Seth. I'd have gone with them but I couldn't be bothered to move. Besides, Ralph and Seth share more of a bond. It's to do with the tattoo Ralph has on his arm. Phil freaked when he first saw it. I knew I recognized it from history classes, but I'd forgotten all that. It didn't really matter to me; the only past I knew, I'd seen on film. Vietnam mostly. Me and Seth used to pretend we'd been there. He'd started having these lucid dreams about it. It's a fucking jungle in there.

'Phil, I can't see it anywhere.' I can never find remote controls in the jungle.

'Then get up. Look, it's there.' He points again.

'Couldn't you just pass it us?'

Ralph had said he wasn't a member any more. That was

from years ago. I really didn't care. Seth said I'd get nowhere without belief. He said, whatever you believe, that's the truth. I look like River Phoenix. I am at one with the animals. Outside, everything is grey.

'What are you putting on anyway?' Phil is picking up the remote control.

'Probably *Platoon*.'

'Oh, fucking hell, no. You watched that four times yesterday.'

'*The Deerhunter*.'

Suddenly *Road Runner* starts up again and catches me by surprise. It even takes me a second to realize it's not actually a cartoon but the phone. I don't have to move to get it.

'Hello.'

Phil looks curious.

'Oh yeah, sure, just pop round.'

Phil looks like a prisoner of war.

'No, I didn't hear it before.'

Phil looks unsurprised.

'OK.' I put the receiver down.

'I presume that was Ralph,' Phil says.

'Yeah, he's coming to pick up the stuff he brought round in that box the other day, thank fuck. He'll be here in a bit. You staying?'

'Nah, nah. I've got to shoot off soonish. By the way, do you know your head's in the ant colony?'

'Yeah, kind of.'

'And you can't be bothered to move it?'

'You just get used to these things I suppose.'

You do. If strangers come into the house they can barely breathe. All of us are chainees and because there are no windows that open in the whole place, well, it's like using a Hoover bag to go scuba diving. Still, you acclimatize to anything. And it keeps the place warm; we can't afford any heating till me and Seth go down the DSS. We've missed about four appointments 'cos he never gets up on time. It's always his fault. The main problem with the fags, though, is that we don't have any ashtrays, so tabs are all floating in half-drunk bottles of old vinegar wine that I'm occasionally tempted to drink, and as extra toppings on pizza, free of charge. The only tray we had is broken on the floor, its old contents blackening a puddle of milk like that Yin and Yang symbol. I rub it all together with my boot.

'Anyway, I'm at one with the animals.'

'They're not animals, they're fucking insects.'

Phil can be so pedantic. I think his little certainties give him something to cling to.

'OK, so I'm at one with the insects, what's the biggy?'

'Didn't you ever see *Starship Troopers*?'

'Yeah, on video the other week, that was the fucking point.'

'Eh?' Phil seems confused.

Confused like chicken boxes. After Ralph had dropped off the box he left straight away. Seth came downstairs looking euphoric and terrified. Just like Christopher Walken. We all wanted to know what was in the box but it took him a while to drag me upstairs. I had to get off my couch. It's real comfortable here, that's why I don't move. I'm not stupid. In fact, I used to be cultured. I know what *The Flight of the Valkyries* sounds like. These days, though, the education comes in embarrassing fits and starts, like my cock. Enough. We left Phil downstairs with a pack of Marlboro Lights and told him to get on with heating duty. It was best he didn't know, then he couldn't worry.

I still don't know how Seth manages to make his room look so exotic. Maybe it's because there's wallpaper. And a carpet. The kind of place you could bring a girl back to. Not that I have her any more. Sorry, one: have one any more. I thought she'd be like a magician's assistant and disappear in the smoke but she never does. Memory, like fate, chooses your life for you and just pulls you along. It's made us all prisoners. That's what got us into this mess in the first place. It wasn't my fault.

'Anyway, what about the bleach down there?' Phil is trying to drag me back from the past into the present.

'What?' It's not going to work. I get the two mixed up at the best of times. The acid flashbacks don't help.

I suppose Seth did it with the throws and perfumes. It never looks like any natural hour in there. It's always the same because he only uses candles and the curtains stay shut. When we went up it was light enough to see, but not enough to show what was there or where you were going. It looked like the insides of your eyelids during a fight, all red and throbbing. When he first pulled open his sock drawer all I could see was socks. Then Seth pulled the whole drawer out of the cabinet and picked up an opaque polythene bag from the space underneath. He passed me the empty KFC box Ralph had brought the package in, told me to take it downstairs, and then opened the bag. I remember breathing the word 'Jesus' and then, 'What are we supposed to do with those?' Seth had this thousand-yard stare on. 'I don't know. Why the fuck do you always expect me to sort out these things? Ralph said he wanted us to hold them for him.' It's not like we could say no. Ralph had used his face to play join-the-dots with scar tissue. He just commanded these things from on high. Seth said, 'They've got to be worth a fortune,' still with that faraway look in his eye. I just worried about getting caught; we'd be looking at about twenty years, I reckoned. Seth simply said, 'I don't intend to get caught.'

Phil has been talking while I've been distracted. I always get distracted; my attention span is fucked these days. I never know what to pay attention to anyway.

'The bleach.' I'm trying to concentrate now. 'Seth couldn't be bothered to get any ant spray so he just covered the holes he thought they were coming out of with bleach.'

'Oh, for fuck's sake.' I suppose I should have been listening. 'What's that meant to achieve?'

'It's Seth, what can you do? It isn't like he's bothered about reason. I think he found it fun watching them melt.'

The rats really got to Seth. He wants to be an exterminator. He says things like, 'That's a career I could be proud of, a real benefit to humanity. I mean who wants pests? That's why they're called pests.' I guess the ants had fallen under his wrath as well.

'How long have I been sleeping in it?'

'I don't know. A few days.'

'Fuck.'

I turn around expecting to see clumps of my film-star hair. I knew there was something in it. Still, it might wash it for me. I suppose the bleach-blue puddles should have stuck out from the browns and the yellows. But the monochrome seeps in from outside. It's best just not to look. And to never have bare feet. They come in in the middle of the night, too groggy to have remembered their shoes, trying to get to the fridge or whatever. We have to cross this place as if it were some mined no-man's land, and leap from chair to chair. Phil came in once – he's quite a big bloke – and he'd stumbled out of his room, climbed on to the arm of the couch, weeble-wobbled a little, jumped and landed on the table. As he tried for the chair by the kitchen he went at it with a bit too much force. The plastic back just snapped, ripped apart like the women in the porn on the walls. I had to cover their bits up with Blu-Tack when the landlady came round. I don't want to offend anyone. Anyway, it all tippled forward till he ended up on his knees in the filth with his nose in this rancid balti, his glasses off and staring up at him from inside the dish covered in something that you were supposed to believe was chicken. You can never be certain.

'Why the fuck didn't anyone tell me before?' I ask.

I can't believe nobody told me about the bleach. Still, I know why they didn't: it was funny. There's no arguing with a joke. You either laugh or you don't. This was funny for them. Funny like falling in filth. Funny like shitting green. Funny like extermination.

'Hey, don't look at me, you're usually asleep when I go out. And it isn't like you to listen,' Phil says.

'I need a fucking drink.'

'There are the wine bottles.' Phil glances at the nicotine-freckled remnants.

'Yeah, great, is there anything else?'

'There are the wine bottles.'

'You said, and it wasn't funny the first time. You don't have to repeat everything.' Nobody in this house can do something just once. That's what got us into this mess in the first place. 'Fuck it. Never mind. A joint'll do.'

'Or you could go and get the housing benefit and everything sorted.'

'Oh fuck off. I'm not moving.' A pause. 'Could you get us a glass of water?'

Phil didn't take the balti incident well. He picked up what was left of the chair and started lobbing it against the wall, over and over, violent as Newton's cradle hit with a golf club, mad like Li Thi had been when we caught her brother violating her cat with a pencil. Phil heard me laughing and turned round, camouflaged and bearded in meat juice. That got me laughing even harder. Seth heard the noise from upstairs, so he came down to destroy things with impunity. It turned into another riot. About half an hour later the pair of them were lighting old copies of the *Sun* and flinging them at the rats. I'd never seen Phil do anything like that before. I just lay there and watched as usual. Actually, I had to leap at one point and dive in front of the TV to save it from a badly thrown bottle.

'When's he getting here?' Phil seems pretty normal now.

'Who?'

'Ralph, you tit, he just phoned. We were talking about it.'

'Oh, yeah. I'd forgotten about that. Pretty soon now. What do you care anyway? And besides we were talking about you getting me a glass of water.'

'Fucksake, can't you do anything for yourself?'

'I'm not going in that kitchen. You've already had the germs. You're, like, immune.'

'But you'll sleep in bleach.'

The bastard is smirking, but he thinks he's so funny that he's gone to get me the water. I lean forward and grab the box to *Apocalypse Now*. We keep all our personal in there so it doesn't get ruined when things are spilled. Newspapers are the worst: five minutes after turning up they're usually on the floor or damp with stains, the black and white just melting into each other. I open the box and pull out all the stuff I need, together with a pack of Prozac from my pocket, and crumble it all up into a Rizla. Believe me, I'm not depressed or anything. Seth takes Viagra with his E and it's not like he struggles to get it up. It's like when Ralph said I looked like I was on heroin. I felt so fashionable. I'm just swinging with the times. As far as I can tell without a clock. Still, they smoke a treat regardless.

'Oh for crying out loud.' Phil is yelling from the kitchen.

'What?'

'There's a rat on top of the washing machine.'

'Yeah . . . And?'

'It's the fucking daytime.'

'They like Coco Pops.'

'What?'

'They do.'

'They're a sign of fucking decay. You don't feed them. That's probably why they're here in the first place.'

'I doubt it.' Sometimes it's all a bit much for him.

'And you certainly don't give them my cereal.'

'They're only your enemies if you make them.'

I've got some doctor friends who usually sort us out with the prescription stuff. They said it shouldn't make any difference, but this Rastafarian fella came round, I think his name was Cornelius, fuck knows how I remember that. Anyway, he was some mate of Ralph's. He brings all kinds round here 'cos we're quiet, we're nobodies, so no one suspects and they can just lie low. Cornelius – he was like this professional getaway driver, seems like they really exist – he said he could feel the difference. He said it felt good. The movies tell me 'Feeling good's good enough.' I'm sure the guy who said that was supposed to be one of the good ones. So I guess it depends who you listen to and how good you are at guessing.

'There are no clean glasses in here.'

'Surprise. There are none in here either.' I presume. 'Next time you go down the pub nick us a few more.'

'Why don't you just fuckin' clean some?'

'Can't you do it?'

'I gotta be going soon.'

I spark up. 'I'm kind of busy.'

Phil comes through with the water. 'Right, I'm off out. I'm working overtime tonight so I probably won't be back till late. Try and keep things under control.' He lights another cigarette.

'Yeah, yeah. See you later.'

Things only really got out of hand when I brought her name up. 'It is funny and then it is no longer funny.' I read that somewhere, when I was fat with books. Seth thought he was helping by saying things like, 'The gooks, they're all cunts.' And I had to say, 'She's not Vietnamese, she's Chinese.' She's not. She's from Dudley. Her mum and dad were. Seth usually says, 'Chinks, dinks, what's the difference?' Then he bangs on about how 'White is right.' It's not worth fighting. There's no questioning faith. She used to get called Bananagirl by some of her mates for going out with me. Yellow on the outside, white on the inside.

The TV is still spewing out a chaos of grey and it's *Friends*. I'm bored of that so I press play on the remote and start the war movie.

Ralph comes straight in through the front door. He doesn't bother knocking these days.

'All right, mate.'

'All right, Ralph, what you been up to?'

'Oh, you know, the usual.'

'Hey, Seth.' I'm shouting but he'll never hear me. I can't be fucked to get up and go to his door. 'Ralph's here.'

'Don't bother waking him up, kid. Just need the stuff 'cos I got some people coming round in an hour or so to pick it up.'

You can't really make small talk with Ralph. Occasionally I'd mention the football, but he just brought the subject round to his old hooligan days.

'Every time, same movies.' Ralph is laughing at me. That never does my anxiety levels any good. Ralph's laughing at me and I can see his teeth that never evolved, never made any progress to brushed fluoride whiteness.

'Here, give us a sec, I'll go and get the gear for you. You want this?' I pass him the joint.

'Cheers, lad.'

The walk upstairs feels like rock-climbing but I get there eventually and bang on Seth's door.

'Mate, Ralph's here.' No answer. 'Mate.' He's bound to still be in bed, sleeping and forgetting like I should be. I push the door open quietly and head for the cabinet, pull open the sock drawer and see nothing but socks. I pull out the whole drawer and there's . . . there's fucking nothing. There's fucking nothing.

'Seth.' Turn on the light. No Seth. *'Seth.'*

There should be something in there. There's got to be something. Look closely. There's fucking nothing.

Downstairs fast like falling. Like Wile E. Coyote off that cartoon cliff.

'It's not my fault. It's Seth.'

'What's the matter, kid?'

'Nothing's up there. I don't know what's going on. I don't know where anything is. Seth's gone.'

'Slow down.' Ralph puts his hand on my shoulder.

I'm breathing like a hacksaw slicing wood.

'Where might he be?' Grip on my shoulder getting harder.

I'm not really listening. There's light in my eyes like diesel on fire. 'I don't know where the bag is. I don't know where Seth's gone.' I think the joint is making my head collapse. I'm panicking. I'm panicking. I hope this is paranoia. I don't know whether I'm guilty or not. I can't remember last night. I can't remember. I don't know.

'I don't know where it is. I don't know where they are.' I don't know what's happening. I'm not used to action. To knives in my throat. Events don't happen. There's a knife at my throat. This can't be happening. I don't take sides. This can't be Ralph. I remember when he showed us a scrapbook of all the cuttings of the times he'd been in the papers. For stabbings and robbings and stuff. It was funny then. It was funny when it was happening to other people. This is not real.

'What do you mean you don't know where it is? What the fuck are you little wankers doing? I need that bag.'

I'm dribbling on him now. Don't do that. Don't do that. That's not going to help. 'Nobody's here. They've all gone and left me. I don't know where it is. I don't know where Seth is.'

'You know what was in that bag? There was fucking twenty grand's worth of E in there.'

'Is that all? I thought it was more than that.' Don't say that. Words dribbling out of my mouth.

'What do you mean, is that fucking all?'

And I'm flying now, flying at the grey walls which have never looked so grey, eyeball to paint, so close it can't be anything, never looked so colourful, all purple bursting awake.

Road Runner is running again. Beeping and beeping in safety and laughter. Loud. So loud now. It must be the phone. It must be Seth. He probably just nipped out. Calling to tell me he's coming back. To get me out of this mess. To tell me this isn't real.

Born to Be Wild

Steve Bishop

I'm looking through my stuff for something to wear in town. The doorbell goes and Mum shouts up from the hall, One of your friends is here, Julian.

I hope it's someone cool like Tom Delaney. Greg told me he goes into town on Saturdays and breaks car aerials and hangs round in the arcade where loads of moody skinhead kids from the estates go; but it's only Martin. He's standing there at the door looking all eager like he's in some stupid American sitcom or something. I can't believe it. OK, so we've sat next to each other in Latin for a couple of years now and done each other's homework from time to time, but that doesn't really qualify as grounds for out of school contact, does it? He's just lucky his dad made a pile with that East Asian stock and got out at the right time. Now they've got a house off Oxford Road, just around the corner from us. Very exclusive – for someone whose dad still drives a Vauxhall Vectra. They used to live in a terraced house in King's Heath till a couple of years ago.

God, he's su-uch a poof. What's he got on his feet, fucking Hi-Tecs? The cheapest Adidas are only a few quid more. Why can't people learn to do things properly? I can't believe he's actually standing there in our doorway in his crappy shoes. And what is that shirt supposed to be? Millets' finest?

It looks like he's planning a full-on house visit, so I say, Suppose you'd better come in then, hoping he'll get the message that I'm only being nice to him 'cos Mum's around. We go through into the kitchen and Mum says, I expect Martin would like a cup of tea, wouldn't he? Of course he would. I'm just starting to really wonder what he's doing here, and he just comes straight out with it: I'm going up to Skye for a week, next weekend, he says. D'you want to come along? And before I can say anything, Mum goes, Ooh, wouldn't that be a nice change? Get you out of the city for a few days, some fresh air in your lungs. You could go canoeing. You used to love canoeing.

You'd think she was dead chummy from the way she talks when other people are around, but it's completely false. If you say what you really want, she waits till whoever it is has gone and then gives you a massive lecture about how you're supposed to behave. She's su-uch a harridan when it comes to manners and all that crap, so I can't just tell him to fuck off to his face. But what makes him think I want to spend a week on some stupid rock in the middle of nowhere with him? I mean, come on. I tell him I've got to finish my project on Robespierre, and then Mum goes and drops me right in it by saying, That hasn't got to be in until the start of the new term. I realize I'm trapped and manage to be polite somehow and tell him it'd be great. Then Mum delivers the *coup de grâce*: Martin's dad has offered you both a lift, so we won't have to worry about trains or anything. Isn't that kind?

So, it seems we're going on holiday. To Scotland. Not exactly cool, but as long as no one from school finds out I don't care. This is their revenge for Thursday night. It wasn't my fault or anything; the old bastards just wouldn't give me any money. I was supposed to be going to a club night in Digbeth called the KittyKat. They do a special pre-late club non-alcoholic bar for under-18s on Thursdays. Everyone from school goes. I was going to meet up with Tom and a few others but Mum got all stroppy and Dad just went to smoke in his study as per usual, so there was nothing doing. I was in a nark anyway because that day at school Tom told me his dad was taking him to the States for the whole summer. He said he'd argued for a place for me, but his dad said that we were a liability when we got together, and in America we'd end up getting shot or something. We had a laugh about that. Some slope-head redneck shooting off shotgun rounds, or chasing us in a flatbed truck with pickaxes and baseball bats.

I went up to my room, locked the door and put on *OK Computer* full blast. That'll teach them to keep me in the house on summer evenings, I thought. I lay on the floor and put the volume up really loud, so the music was vibrating through me. It feels amazing – like being in a room with the band playing all around you. My stereo's cool. I got it for my fourteenth. It's a Sony. It's got fifty watts per channel. If it wasn't for that I'd have left this dump ages ago. I'd've gone to live with someone from school who's got cool parents. It can happen: Tom Delaney said he lived with Scott Bainbridge for a whole two months after he went for his dad with a pair of garden shears.

When the record finished, I could hear Dad through the door going, I want to have a serious word with you, Julian. So I told him to fuck off. It felt really dangerous, like something out of a film. I had the door locked so he just went away. Next morning he was all serious, not that he's ever any other way. They locked up my stereo and said I could have it back when I could act a bit more like an adult. I said I thought that was how adults acted.

So, after all that, the stupid rock in the middle of nowhere is probably meant to be 'good for me' or something. It might not be so bad. At least there won't be any parental hassles and I can get some serious smoking and drinking done. And Mum will be so chuffed that I'm going away with poofy Martin instead of bad-boy Tom, maybe if I act 'good' for a bit she'll give me loads of dosh.

Mum goes, Right, I'll leave you two to sort out the details, and goes to hack up some veg in the back-kitchen. I look at Martin and say, I'm OK with this as long as you don't go around school telling everyone.

– Why would I do that? he says, laughing a bit and rolling his eyes, but I can tell he's a touch pissed off. – Don't worry, I won't spoil your cool image or anything.

– Well, just as long as we understand each other.

– I didn't know you could canoe.

– I can't.

– But your mum said –

– Just drop it, all right?

The end of the last day of term. It's a tough hurdle. Martin's been taking the piss all week, coming up to me with the pretext of having some work to swap or a conjugation issue. He hasn't mentioned going on holiday, but I can feel the tension when he's around. I know he wants to tell people and make out he's a mate and everything. Everyone's piling out of the place for the summer. I swapped numbers with lucky bastard Tom, and said I'd ring him at his parent's condo in Miami. And Greg's off to the South of France. They're going over on the Eurostar in his dad's new Aston Martin. Fucking minted they are. Tom goes, I'm bringing a gun back from the States.

– Oh yeah, I say, sure you'd get that through Customs.

– I'm getting a Glock, he says. – They're plastic. The machines won't pick it up.

I'll believe it when I see it. But just imagine how cool that would be. Walking round going, Are you looking at me? Are you looking at me? CDs are half the price over there and you can get Levi's and Gap clothes for almost nothing. I ask Tom to get me some combats, but he tells me there's a weight limit.

I look round and there's this blob kind of sidling up to me. Martin. Oh fuck, he's going to give the game away. He'd better not even dare mention it in front of my real friends. Thinking quickly, I go, See ya boys, and pushing past Martin I slap him on the back and say, in a friendly sort of a way, So long Fatso! Dad's at the gates as I sprint up all sweaty. Martin, to his credit, hasn't followed me, which is just as well 'cos the boys are looking over to check out my exit. I wish Dad would replace the BM. Everyone's got them nowadays.

– Would your friend Martin like a lift?

– No, no, his dad's coming to meet him, let's go.

Close one. It's not like Martin's persona non grata or a total jinx or anything, it's just that he's not cool in any way.

Martin's dad looks like Jesus. He's got one of those close-cropped beards that George Michael had ten years ago and collar-length hair that looks like it might actually have – gasp – highlights, except it's just his stupid hair getting sun-bleached. When he came to pick me up this morning I thought he was some sort of charity worker come to collect for Help the Aged or something. I nearly yawned in his face. Then he said, Hi, I'm Gerry, your chauffeur for the day, and laughed at his own joke. I wondered what he was on about for a minute; I was still a bit sleepy. I'd been up most of the night reading *On the Road*. Then the penny dropped. Today I'm going to nerdsville with the bores.

I scrunch down into the back seat. Martin did offer me

the front, but though it's more comfy there's not much cover in case anyone sees me, and I'd be sitting next to Jesus, which would be hard to explain. Fortunately, Martin's dad seems content to subject us to Jethro Tull or whatever hippie shite it is that he's into and I'm spared having to be polite. He takes the Alcester Road out of Moseley and into town for the motorway. Fortunately there's no one about. Once we hit the inner ring road I start to relax a bit and sit up. It's not such an uncomfortable car if you sit in it properly, but I'm still trying to get used to the idea that I'll be sitting here with Martin and his dad for the next six hours. Just as I'm about to get comfy, maybe read *The Face*, Martin turns round and says, D'you want to play Travel Scrabble? It's like a nightmare. I'm trapped in a mobile prison for geeks. Now he's getting out the sandwiches. They're cut into little triangles and not a crust in sight. I look in his Karrimor rucksack, which is laid out on the back seat next to me (for me to lie on if I get tired later). Everything in it is in little plastic bags so it won't get wet if it rains. This is all topped off with a Gore-Tex coat, which is probably his idea of fashion. All I've got is some Gap gear I just threw into a sportsbag along with the tinnies. I hope it doesn't rain, 'cos it'll be really ugly having to wrestle his posh raincoat off him. I've only got a Levi's denim jacket and it's not very waterproof.

Just as we get out on the motorway up past Cannock and towards Stafford, it starts to piss down; sheets of heavy rain sluice across the car with the wipers going schlack, schlack across the windscreen. Headlights go on and I lie back on Martin's comfy rucksack and imagine the car aquaplaning across a huge skidpan, floating over the tarmac, and ascending into space. By the time I wake up it's bright sunshine again and we're up in Cumbria somewhere. That's great. I've managed to sleep about half the journey. I turn over and try to get back to sleep for the rest of the way but it's no good. I stare out of the side window, not letting the other two know I'm awake so I don't have to speak to them. Next to my head there's a huge sound, an engine. This guy on a motorbike comes past so quick all I get is a glimpse of matt black helmet and flapping clothes. Then there's a whole load more of them, thirty, fifty even. They ride past like they were the only thing on the road. It's like *Mad Max* or something out there.

Gerry drops us at the campsite and gets the rest of the stuff from the boot. There's no going back now. I'm stuck with this for a week. I'll just have to make the best of it. It's raining a bit and a good two degrees colder than it was in Birmingham. I've got plenty of supplies to keep me going and a couple of books if the worst comes to the worst. Gerry gives Martin a hug and we wave goodbye in the swirling drizzle.

The campsite is almost on the beach. There's a sort of little cliff that dips right down to the shore. It's stony down there though, not sand. I ask Martin, Are you disappointed you can't make sandcastles now? He giggles and starts doing poofy things like putting tents up. I empty his rucksack out and demolish the rest of the sandwiches. They're quite good if you eat them three at a time. I'm still really hungry so I get the stove and my asparagus and Stilton soup out. Then Martin goes, Let's go skinny dipping. He's already out of his shorts and flinging them over the top of the tent. I shout after him, I'll tell everyone back at school you've exposed yourself to me on a remote Scottish island.

This gets a big laugh from him and he strips off his top and runs into the water, with his fat arse wobbling across the shingle. The water looks freezing – serves him right – and grey if you get up close. It's really quite nippy up here in the breeze and the sun has almost disappeared under the horizon. I haven't even taken my jacket off since I got out of the car. I hand Martin his towel when he comes back. He's blue, the mad bastard; you have to admire his guts. He gets out this duck-down sleeping bag from a neat little package that looks more like it's got a mac in it than a sleeping bag.

I lie back and crash out in the tent for a bit and the next thing I know it's getting light again and I'm woken up by boiling sun in the tent. The last of the flask tea is gone and I'm fucking starving. The shop's miles away, so I show Martin my little holiday present to myself. I hold it out for him to have a look at and sniff. I paid a whole week's allowance for it. Twenty-five quid it cost. Martin asks me if I really paid twenty-five for it, as if he can't believe that drugs could be that cheap, but it's money well spent if it's as good as it's supposed to be. I got it at school off Scott Bainbridge. I had to give Tom a whole pack of fags before he'd even introduce me to him.

I think Martin's well impressed. He must've thought pot was dead expensive, like cocaine. He keeps going, Twenty-five quid for a tenth, and laughing like he can't believe it. I get the papers and tobacco out and we roll cigarettes to put it in, but it's difficult to get the paper to roll around and seal up like it's supposed to. Then Martin goes, On the Woodstock film, one of the hippies makes a pipe out of tinfoil, so we give that a try. He gets this KitKat wrapper, all chocolaty still, and we make it into a pipe pretty easily and the pot crumbles into it from the lighter with only a couple of burnt fingers. I put the pipe to my mouth, put the lighter to the pot and take a deep breath. I nearly cough my guts up, choking for about five minutes afterwards; it's mad.

I gulp down some Lucozade and try not to sneeze it down my nose from laughing so much. I drag myself out of the tent and into the field, lying on my back in the long grass and looking at the sky. It's still clear, the sun right overhead. It seems like late afternoon, but my whole sense of time seems foreshortened. This is the first time I've thought about it since we left Birmingham. There's this chugging sound coming across the island and up into the field. Like an old aeroplane or something. Martin says, What's that? So I tell him it's some old guy from the village come to take him on a date and show him the sights and sounds of the island. The gate into the field opens and a middle-aged man with a greying ZZ Top beard comes in on a motorbike, a real oldie one without any plastic mouldings or anything. It would look really cool if there wasn't some weirdo riding it.

We watch him as he starts putting his tent up. I can't help cracking up. He looks so funny, like a Smurf or something. Motorbike Smurf, with his comedy beard. There's this picture on the back of his jacket, like a skull with wings on it. Why do old people still try to be cool? I think, Why can't they just face it and be old? I tell Martin it's the ferryman's hairy bumchum and later they're going to make beautiful cheese together.

– D'you know what that picture means on his back? he says.

– It means he's an arse bandit, I say.

– No, it means he's a Hell's Angel.

– Don't be stupid, they're only in films, there aren't any real ones any more.

– Yes there are, I saw a film about them on BBC2.

– I'm going to make another spliff.

– I dunno . . .

– Come on, don't be lame.

I build my own and so does Martin. We agree that it's gross to put your mouth where someone else's has been. That would be a PCO: personal contact offence. Rack more than three of those up in a term and you're a poof for ever. Now I'm curious about bikers, so I ask Martin, What was on this programme then?

– Loads of stuff, he says. – They're really mad. They get all their money from making their girlfriends into prostitutes, and they deal loads of drugs.

– Bullshit.

– No, it's true, honestly. They went through all this stuff that you have to do to be a Hell's Angel, like wear a pair of jeans that have been soaked in the whole gang's piss for a week. Then they beat the crap out of you and you have to take it to prove that you're dead hard. And then you have to get chased across town on your bike by the police and outrun them.

– Sounds like school only a bit more hardcore.

– Quite a bit more.

– Let's have a smoking contest.

– Huh?

– Yeah, come on, see who can take the most.

– What's the point? It can just be for relaxing, you know. It doesn't have to be for frying your brain all the time.

I manage to persuade him, and we cane our way through an entire spliff each before crashing out, completely smashed. Lying on my back again, looking at the cloud formations, I hear all this rustling in the grass behind me like he's moving around to get more comfy, and then there's a breeze as he gets up. Martin is bounding over to the hole in the ground that's supposed to be our bog, leaning over it and absolutely hurling his ring. I swear, I've never seen anything so funny.

He comes limping back, looking all pale and going on about white worms. The little bastard had food all along and had a tin of cold spaghetti for lunch. There's a load more food in his rucksack. The only problem is it's the sort you have to cook. I try to get the stove to work. Some more tea, maybe a bacon butty. There's this canister and a sort of burner thing that goes over the top of it and these clips that are supposed to go over the sides, but they don't fit, and when I eventually get them on, no gas comes out. After I've spent about ten minutes putting the damn thing together, Martin – looking a bit less green – comes and tells me I've got to put a hole in the top of the canister myself, so I undo the whole thing again, which isn't easy, and stick a fork in the top of the can. Before I can put it all back together, this gas comes spraying out and I try to get the burner bit on the top but the pressure of the gas is too strong and when I push down on it all this white liquid gas stuff comes out all over my hands. So I say to Martin, half taking the piss, What do I do now, just light it then? Martin nearly craps himself, and goes, Give it here, I'll do it.

But he's just as useless. I can't stop laughing. The fact that Martin doesn't think it's at all funny makes it even funnier. After he's been pissing about with it for about a minute and given up in exasperation, I ask him, What do we do now then, brains? And he says, I dunno, why don't you sniff the rest of the butane?

– Bloody hell, Martin, that's a bit rock'n'roll for you, isn't it? I say. And I give it a go. It's amazing. Everything goes all purple and green and I feel dead dizzy. Martin starts looking like a cartoon version of himself. I lie on my back and look at the sky, and there's all these images of people dancing about above my head. I suppose that's where people get their ideas for music videos and stuff like that.

The next thing, Martin's telling me he was only kidding when he said to sniff the butane, and you could die from that, and the only people who sniff things are from council estates. Martin starts going on about wanting some food so we set off for the village up the road. The sun's out and we walk quite fast. Martin's full of the joys of the great outdoors; I'm still buzzing off the gas. You can smell the heather and sea, all perfume and ozone. We boot Martin's soft football down the road. It's good to be able to do that and know there's probably not a car for miles.

The shop stinks of mould and old people. There's this bell above the door on a spring. It's like going back into history. I'm nearly laughing just at that, then I catch sight of the old git in his overall with his dungarees. He's smoking a pipe. Martin's getting all huffy all of a sudden. I think it must be because I'm laughing at the fishy old Santa Claus. He's trying to buy everything and get out quick, so I ask the old guy for some worms, just to piss Martin off. It's not like I'm even doing anything that bad – I really would like to do a bit of fishing. I bet there's some massive carp in the deep pool over the other side of the rocks. Better than Pot Noodle for tea anyway. Then I ask for some white worms and Martin goes scarlet, tells me to shut up. I'm sure that his top lip's trembling. The old guy tells me they're just ordinary worms, but it shouldn't be a problem and there were sharks off the coast last summer and rich Yanks came over from the grouse shoots to fish them. I nod with sarcastic wisdom. The old guy tells me to watch out for the incoming tides if I'm on the sandbar and lends me an old fishing rod. He was all right after all. By the time I get outside, Martin has lightened up a bit and we have a laugh about the old chap in the shop giving it to his sheep, with its back legs tucked into his wellies.

When we get back, Martin's a bit reluctant to skin up again, but then I offer him some of mine (after wiping the end of course). We're lying on our backs in the grass and there's this sound of an engine getting louder and louder; a fishing boat maybe? Too loud for that. It could be a Hercules plane or something. I give Martin a look to see if he's realized what it is as well. He looks like he's crapped himself. It's about a hundred motorbikes, all kinds of shapes, and sizes from big to massive. Most of them are Harleys or Triumphs.

They look wicked; all gleaming chrome, fat tyres, flaming or sparkling paint jobs, some of them much rougher looking, but still just as cool. The bikers are all wearing leather, shiny or matt, with open-face helmets and goggles. The noise is unbelievable. It goes past your ears and hits your chest like a hammer. Some of them are pulling skids up the other end of the field. One guy comes past with his biker chick hanging off the back, facing backwards. She licks her tongue out at Martin and blows him a kiss.

– Does that mean she wants to shag me? His voice leaps an octave.

– Yes, Martin, she's going to make you a man. It'll cost you though.

I remind him that all their girlfriends are prostitutes and that's how they get money. Perhaps they put them in porno mags and movies – every porno mag I've ever seen has women like that in it. They all have long straight hair, wear nothing but maybe a pair of cowboy boots and lie over the back seat of a Harley Davidson. The girls probably sit round the campfire at night, taking their clothes off and showing their bits to the men. Then Martin says, They might make us shag them so we get AIDS like them.

– How d'you know they've got AIDS?

– Well they're prostitutes, aren't they?

One of the bikers is chucking an axe around. They're throwing them at each other and drinking beer out of these little barrels. It looks really cool, but I do kind of wish they were at a safer distance. Martin starts to panic. He wants to leg it. He thinks they're going to come and start chucking axes at him too. One of them's got an iron cross. Martin says that means they're Nazi bikers. They're spinning their bikes round in circles and pulling wheelies and stuff.

– Nazi bikers tie people between two bikes and then pull them in half!

– Shut up, Martin, stop stressing me out! No one's getting pulled in half. Target practice maybe . . .

One of them drags a load of logs up to the middle of where they are and pours petrol all over them. He whips out a Zippo and they go up with a whoosh.

– That's their sacrificial pyre, I say. – No one knows we're here, Martin.

– The old guy at the shop.

– He's probably the high priest!

I'm almost physically restraining him from running off across the beach. I tell him, They'll still get you, Martin. They like a moving target. If we stay still they might not see us.

– Oh Jesus. Fuck.

– Fuck, too late. One of them's seen us, he's coming over.

This fucking, like, man-mountain comes striding over. He's seven feet tall at least with blond hair down to his waist. He looks like something out of *Xena Warrior Princess* or one of those crappy old Dungeons and Dragons films that Martin and his geek squad are into. Martin tells me he's going to make a run for it.

– We can't now. They've seen us. They'll chuck axes at us.

– Oh God, I just hope they don't tie us between two bikes.

– Or burn us alive.

Like a reflex we dive into the tent and get under the covers. Martin says, I'm not fucking anyone who's got AIDS.

– Or sharing any dirty needles.

About ten seconds later the tent shakes like it's going to fall down.

– Oh fuck, he's outside! What do we do?

– Go see what he wants.

– He might chop my head off!

– Shut up, shut up, he'll hear you.

– You go.

– No, you go. You're the host, it's your tent.

Then the mad, murderous Nazi biker goes, Orroight, mate, 'zit OK if we borrow the footie ferra bit?

– Er . . . Yeah, of course. Martin hands him the football and comes back in and starts hassling me. – You're shaking, he goes, like he was my mum or something.

– No I'm not, I say, I'm just shivering. Close the tent, will you, it's cold. He keeps asking me if I'm all right so in the end I have to say, Of course I'm all right. I'm not a fucking mummy's boy like you, you know. So then he has to sulk all evening.

I'm making Martin do one of his horrible tinfoil pipes while I do some hot knives off a milk bottle. It's great weather again. I feel really energetic and Martin seems to have forgotten all about last night's panic attack, so we play football on the beach. The bikers put the ball back by our tent along with a can of Helgenbrau. Two bikers come across the sand from the huge tent thing they've put up at the edge of the beach and join us.

– Noice one, mate, one says. – We shoulda brought a footie 'n' all.

We start kicking the ball around. Then a couple more bikers come to join in the game. They're glad that we're both Blues fans, and now so are we. Another couple of guys come over and make goals out of jackets. Pretty soon, me and Martin are captaining opposing teams of bikers amid flying hair and rasping leather, shouts of Man on! and Cross it, ya dick'ead! I don't want to catch Martin's eye. I'm not sure if it's just the pot or the weirdness of the situation, but I have to concentrate on the game to stop myself from collapsing in hysterics. Me and Martin, each captains of full eleven-men teams of Hell's Angels, playing football on some field in the middle of nowhere, beach on one side, mountains on the other, stoned out of our heads. I never thought in a million years that I would ever be doing anything like this. My team wins, 6–4.

The bikers leave for a burn around the island, doing a bit of exploring. I ask to go along, but they tell me there's no room, so we're left behind. I'm starving, but all the food's been eaten and dingbat Martin's left the milk in the sun and it's gone off. We're both still hungry. Martin's on about the shop again. Fuck that, I say, I'm going to catch a shark. I check the canister for more butane, but it's quite low. I must have used a lot doing hot knives. It wasn't my fault, I kept dropping the knives and before I could get everything else ready they'd gone cold again.

There's a huge sandbar a couple of hundred yards out so I wade into deeper water. The sea's dead still. There must be at least some decent flatfish, if not sharks. I stick the worms on the hook and cast off, sending the line zipping out into the blue. It's good just to be standing out there. My legs are tired after the football, so I borrow Martin's inflatable chair. I couldn't believe it when he got it out and started pumping it up with a bike pump. I told him it was for poofs whose bums are too sensitive to sit on grass. It's well comfy, though. I could do with a beer. In the sun, I'm sleepy again. I'm just drifting off when I get a bite. I pull on the line like mad, trying to wheel the fish in. It's really strong, definitely a shark, maybe a blue shark washed up from the Med or something. Martin's shouting encouragement from the beach. The fish is thrashing around in the water, making all these little waves. I pull the line back and push the lever round, trying to get the winder thingy an extra couple of notches round. Martin's still shouting. He sounds really keen – I reckon the shop must've been shut and he wants his tea. With a massive ping something snaps and the fish is gone. I nearly snap the rod over my knee in frustration.

I go to pick up Martin's chair and find that it's been washed away by the tide, which has come in behind the sandbank and is now slopping at my heels. I wade over back towards the shore. Martin's still on the shoreline, waving and yelling, and for the first time I can make out why he's shouting.

– You're cut off, you dickhead. You'll fucking drown if you try to swim across now.

– No I won't. Just 'cos you're a physical wreck and you couldn't swim the length of a bathtub.

I wade about halfway across and suddenly I'm waist deep in this current that's so strong it's nearly pushing me off my feet. The water that looked really calm from a distance is all rippled because it's moving so fast. If I go any deeper I know I'll lose my footing. So I tell Martin, Get your fat arse over here, will you? He comes about as close as he dares, nearly getting swept away himself. We're standing about two metres apart, and between us is this immense water. Then he goes, Pass me the rod. So I send one end of it over to him, he keeps hold of it and I launch myself into the water which swings me round at right angles to the beach straight away. Water splashes past me like I was water-skiing or something. Somehow Martin keeps hold of the rod and stays on his feet. I work my way along the rod, using the little loops as grips and kicking with my feet. Eventually I get far enough to be able to stand up again on the other side and we drag ourselves through the water to the beach, exhausted.

Suddenly it all just seems so funny. I never felt more like laughing in my life. I don't know why. Maybe it's just relief at not being drowned or washed away into some deep offshore sea-pool. Then Martin goes, You mad bastard, you nearly died then.

– Yeah, that was pretty rock'n'roll, I say.

Martin looks at me like I'm mental or something. Then he

starts laughing too. He's all right, Martin, really, once you get to know him.

I think his worst fault, his only real fault, actually, if you ignore his total disregard of fashion, is that he's got no clue about context. First day back at school and we're outside assembly, just waiting for the bell so we can file into the hall for the usual crap about how we have to work hard and behave and all that and Martin comes bounding up to me and goes, Hi, Julian, what are you doing after school? How about going to the arcade? Like I'm his best buddy or something. I've never been so-o embarrassed. Tom's standing right next to me and goes, Ha! You've been hanging out with fatboy. And all I can think of as a comeback is, He lives round the corner from me, what can I do? Right in front of him, which, fortunately, Tom finds hilarious. I feel a bit of a bastard but what can I do? He's not speaking to me now. And he's sitting next to John Amesbury in Latin. I don't care. I sit next to spacker Harrison and draw pictures of him dribbling. It makes everyone laugh anyway.

A Death in the Family

David Savill

During his lunch hour, Ryan discovered that his dad was having an affair. He'd been buying a Mother's Day card, of all things, at the Disney Store: *Beauty and the Beast* swinging from the bells of Notre-Dame. He was already on the escalator before he spotted them and hopped back against the crowds to stay hidden. Gravity collapsing beneath him, Ryan watched over the silver railings of the mezzanine; shouts and laughter drowned in his throbbing head. It was difficult to say how he knew something was going on between them: the way she giggled nervously; a look he had never seen on his father's face, eyes blind with desire. In those eyes the uncut lawns of April, the unwashed car, the reminders for bills all made sense. Three weeks ago, without a word to anyone, Ryan's dad had quit the Rotary Club.

His father and the girl sat there a full ten minutes, by a carbonate stork frozen in paint-blue water beneath plastic palms. She was really quite attractive, lively ringlets of hair and upper lip arched like a duck's bill. Beauty and the Beast.

– Yam late, said Darren when Ryan got back to work.

Ryan stared through his floor manager and apologized,

barely registering the situation. Darren was covering Ryan's till, something he hated doing on account of his size. Behind the till he was just a head to the customers, a good few inches shorter than Ryan even with his two-year seniority. But Darren managed by fear; born and bred in Dudley, built like a castle wall. On Ryan's first day he'd seen Darren disciplining another new member of staff for voiding a transaction without seeking supervisory permission. Darren was in the smoking room, the other side of the glass partition, slapping the lad. Kumar was so fresh he took it like a child does from his parents; just looked hurt and walked off. Darren looked at Ryan and silently mouthed 'Yeah?' The walls and windows of the smoking room were yellow and Darren looked like the devil from anti-smoking ads he'd watched as a kid. With Darren, emotional excuses would not wash.

Ryan took over the till and thought about how to ask for Sunday off but, as with most things, the decision was thrust upon him. In the toilets, he found Darren levelling one rolled up shirt sleeve with the other. Here was a man who lived company policy, who took pleasure in interpreting wage slips and calculating holidays owed. Ryan's shift the next day was supposedly voluntary. He decided that this was his best angle.

– Bu' yer said jus' Wednesday yow wur desperate t'wurk Sunday fur the extra cash. Yow've wurked fur us how long, Ryan, August? Tha' manes yow've dun six munths and accrued sixteen days' leave.

Ryan hesitated to state the obvious but marched on Darren's heels through to the lingerie department.

– Which means I've got nine days left, right?

Darren stood in front of a wall-sized promotional poster advertising the new line in black basques. The model loomed seductively above him blowing a kiss.

– Actulloi, twelve days includin' statutory, bu' tha' aye gor nuthin' to do with your 'avin Sunday off. Yam rotored on –

– But I thought it was voluntary?

– The rotor aye voluntary. Yam rotored on and yow've a week's notice to give 'fore yer can change it. Darren widened his eyes to dare an answer.

Storming off, Ryan caught a bra strap on his cuff and let it fall to the floor. Stage two supervisor was still a year of jumper folding away; second-rate job, second-rate place, second-rate dad. He was still in a mental argument with Darren when he finished his shift and left Merry Hill. The bus back to Birmingham was stuck behind lorries carrying soil from the quarries of phase three of the centre's development. He was an hour late home and the city darkness had fallen.

The next morning, Ryan wasn't even sure if he had slept. He sweated beneath the duvet and lay in wait for the alarm to flick over to 9.30, visualizing Lynn putting her headset on. He picked up the phone from the shagpile carpet of his studio flat and concentrated on swallowing.

It could be flu, everyone else had been off with it.

The store answering machine started up before Lynn cut in. Ryan didn't know where the opening croak in his voice had come from. Maybe he really was ill.

She broke him off. – Absence calls have to go directly to the floor manager. Putting you through, Ryan.

– No! He put his head in the pillow and waited on the silence. – I mean, Darren's not in today.

– I've still got to put you through to the acting manager.

He heard the extension number start ringing then put the phone down. He really was sick after all. He was doing the right thing staying at home.

Ryan stared at the ceiling and concentrated on how he felt: a faint buzzing headache, but only the kind you get from watching too much television or standing under artificial lights all day, staring at computerized till screens. He dreamed his way into sleep, riding a story about the small claims court and compensation for health risks in the workplace. They handed him a cheque worth two years' wages and he bought everyone in the pub a round of drinks – including her from furnishings – before flying out to Australia, where he doubled his money in property investment. He sent his parents a postcard of a strange place on the edge of a red rocky mountain; his dad ripped it up . . .

He woke in a panic. He had slept on his left arm and lost all feeling. Turning over, he waited long seconds before the blood began to flow, unable to lift the arm from his bedsheets. As sensation returned, he touched his face with numbed clubs of fingers, trying to take a temperature or at least recognize the contours. Flu, he thought, and felt heavy in breath. He was sick, sick, sick.

Morning tipped in and out of the gap between brown curtains; a thin stream of blue light spilled through, trembling in the radiator's rising heat.

Ryan propped himself up and thought of the day's possibilities. The blood rushed from his head and he realized he probably just wasn't used to being in bed so long with the heating on.

Nursed by a cup of tea, he let light into the room and stood in corners of the room he hadn't tried before, looking for a different angle on things. He showered, then wiped condensation off the kitchenette cupboard mirror and made crazy faces until his eyes began to pop out of his head. He was a mad Maori, a dark spirit.

If you stared at yourself long enough you could become someone else.

He made up the sofabed in the lounge and unsuccessfully hoovered the carpet; he emptied the bag and the Hoover gave him double the suction it ever had, made football-pitch stripes on the deep brown shagpile. He dusted the old record player and put on a Bluetones LP, then cleaned the inside of the windows and dusted the plants. Watching shafts of dust come alive in the sunshine, he decided the room needed hoovering again. Stripes in the opposite direction this time. It made the room look bigger. He switched on the TV and was surprised to find that it was 11.33 and they were well into religious programming.

The local news was less depressing. Flooding out at Worcester where a riverside landlord was sitting on a barstool, the Severn brown and self-satisfied around his knees. A cricketer bowled spin, chopping through the ankle-deep tide; a close-up of the ball bobbing towards the wickets. Birmingham was to have a one million pound street festival to celebrate the millennium: industrial exhibits to celebrate the past and a multicultural carnival to usher in the future. At least that's what the presenter said. He wore an authoritative moustache and the suit of an entrepreneur uncle. Finally, there had been a killing at a place called Hawes Lane: shots of a bus stop and redbrick church against a heathland estate. The report was read over the same three shots in circular succession; only the camera angles were slightly different. A short pan of the exhaust-blackened Methodist church and a still of the pavement, damp in places with windswept daffs. A shotgun had been involved; no leads so far.

Ryan picked up the remote and switched the TV off. Time to go out, make something of the stolen day.

He was boiling the kettle for coffee when Darren rang.

Sunday at the Merry Hill Centre was twice as depressing as any other day. He took the shuttle bus packed with families. He watched a toddler on her mother's lap making handprints on the steamed up windows then putting her finger on her mother's lips, who licked away the condensed breath. Long queues into the centre. Ryan was already three hours late for work. Purring smugly, the bus sat beneath defunct monorail lines. No one opened a window and the bus slowly became engulfed in a cloud of other people's breath. Ryan felt suffocated; he asked the driver to let him out and walked across the car park, trying to cut as straight a line as possible through the crowded lot.

Darren put him on clean-up duty, trailing around after customers who couldn't fold T-shirts. The store manager seemed to be keeping an eye on him and Ryan was convinced Darren was taking dresses off their hooks, dropping them to test his vigilance.

Break didn't come until half three. He went and sat by the stork pond where he'd seen his dad with the girl and took the lid off a triple-pack BLT. The tomatoes had soaked into the bread. He dipped his fingers into the lukewarm water of the pond. A transparent skin tipped the stagnant surface. After only a few years the whole place was shoddy. You noticed these things when you worked there. The paint on the stork was scratched, corroded tin beneath its wings.

Up by the silver railings where he'd been standing the day before, a skinny young mother was yanking the arm of her child, almost lifting the puppet feet of the screaming toddler from the ground. It took Ryan straight back to when he'd been thirteen, his mum in a rage, shaking a piece of white paper and blowing everything out of proportion. OK, so he'd lied to friends at school that it was his birthday. He'd lied to Sarah Cardigan, a private white lie to get her attention, and before he knew it he'd had to tell everyone. All he'd got from Sarah was a look and a smile but by the end of the day the whole year was wishing this boy they hardly knew a happy birthday. Celia, a girl from two years below, popped a hand-made birthday card through his letter box, just a folded piece of paper without an envelope. His mother stared straight at him with the paper in her hand, shouting in disbelief that her own son could be a liar. And all Ryan could think was that her mouth screwed up in anger looked exactly like a dog's arse, that she should get a life and stop shaming herself in front of him. Pretty much from that moment, it seemed as if he had never stopped noticing signs of age in her face and hair and shrinking body. He felt sorry for his mum and for her ugliness. That Mother's Day he'd taken her to the Botanical Gardens. He insisted on paying for everything out of his own pocket money, the entrance fee, the tea, the ice-cream that she licked in the jungle palm hothouse. He could see her mouth now, tongue swiping at the Mr Whippy, and how he'd turned up his nose when she offered it to him.

On the bus home someone had left a copy of the *Birmingham Post*. It was celebrating the Midland's heroic mothers in a double-page spread; mothers who had saved their children from burning houses, a paraplegic mum who'd raised five kids on her own when her husband left her. The murder on Hawes Lane made front-page headlines. A schoolboy, 16, had been shot as he waited for the bus home after his evening class. The police were stumped for a motive, although witnesses said at least two youths had fled the scene on foot. The front page ran the same pictures that Ryan had seen on the local news. A deep-focus shot with flowers in the foreground and a redbrick Methodist church looking sinister on the skyline. He had seen that church somewhere, he recognized the wrought-iron gates with a crucifix woven into the pattern and the patch of bare heath just visible beyond a castle turret. It was a solid, industrial-age church without a spire, not like the middle England C of E he'd been to as a child. He put the paper back where he'd found it. The six o'clock sky behind abandoned mining wheels was shocking pink from the spires of Brierley Hill to the silhouette of Dudley Castle. Over Birmingham everything was an unnatural white – whiter than white. Beautiful pollution. They were stuck in a jam on the brow of Dudley Hill and he was half an hour late home.

– Where's me card then? his mother asked when he phoned, but Ryan could tell she was happy to hear from him, there was a smile in her voice. He told her it was sitting next to the kettle and she'd have to come round for tea if she wanted to get it.

– How's Dad? he asked.

– Oh, yer dad's yer dad.

He thought about it through the night. Up at two a.m., he looked in the fridge: nothing but a tub of Stork and a plastic bag of mushrooms. He tried to think of a good combination, but couldn't get his head round the fact there were only two ingredients. The buzzing freezer element fluctuated in his ears, like a ship's engine hum keeling over waves. He stared into the light of the fridge until his mind began to sleep, until he thought that closing the door and turning round might take him back to breakfast at home.

Late to work the next day, Ryan was punished with Goods In, taken off the shop floor for leaving it like a bombsite on Sunday. Apparently Darren knew just what a bombsite was like because he'd seen it all with the Territorials.

Deliveries were made in a titanic underground loading bay that serviced the entire centre. Lorries backed up and unloaded into the four bays designated to Marks & Spencer. Racks of suits and summer collections were wheeled off, clothes made for a sun he didn't seem to see much of these days. Everything in Goods In smelled of dry cleaning and the rotten sickliness of decomposing cardboard. Daylight only broke in with a new truck, blinding until the entrance shutters were slammed down. An orange fog drifted around in the metal roof beams: petrol fumes and fags. Workers in other loading bays were going about their business of shifting and lifting or just standing around smoking, skin blanched in the orange lights. Behind these were the barcoders, the beeps of their machines like electronic crickets echoing into the vast space.

Kumar was working in Goods In, running his barcoder over packets of ties. He had a dump bin of them, about a thousand to work through. Ryan told Kumar he thought he'd left the company.

– Na, mate, I prefer it down 'ere. Keep out of everyone's way.

– Starting to like retail then?

– Retail is retail is retail, man.

Ryan picked up his barcoder and ran it across a triple pack of paisley Y-fronts. He did six hundred Y-fronts before lunch, when he stormed to a payphone and dialled his dad's carphone number.

– Hello, Ryan! I'm on bu . . . and . . . is it anyway?

Ryan visualized his dad's voice being broken by passing trucks, motorway bridges, satellite debris.

– It's a bad signal, Dad. I'll call you back.

– But I ca . . . you perfectly.

– Dad, I can't hear you properly. I'm on a payphone, I'll ring back.

– That's fun . . . understand . . . I can hear loud and clear.

A woman in a Boots uniform stood a polite distance from Ryan. When he looked round she smiled demonstratively, like a children's TV presenter. Isn't life a wonderful voyage of discovery? her smile seemed to say.

– Ju . . . and say wha . . . ou want, his dad was saying.

– Fuck it! Ryan shouted. – I've run out of money. He slammed the phone down.

The Boots girl gave a sympathetic grimace. *Sandra,* her badge said. *Cosmetics.*

Ryan didn't speak to anyone after that until Graham phoned in the evening to ask him down the Hare and Hounds. Opening his mouth to answer, Ryan wasn't sure whether his voice box would function properly. Seven hours he had been silent, he counted; it had become a sort of challenge.

There was a band called Sonique Ferrets playing. Graham sort of knew the singer, said they were a kind of mix between old French film music and hardcore punk – moogified and thrashy. Graham was trying to round up the lads. It would have been easy to tell Graham about his dad but Ryan didn't feel like coping with his reaction. Graham would swear in a long drawn out way, searching for the right words, then ask him whether he wanted to do something quiet tonight, talk about it. If Ryan said yes it would secretly piss Graham off; he'd come round and they'd open cans and talk about anything except the situation. Graham would be distant all night and eventually try to persuade him to go and catch the end of Sonique Ferrets. He was Ryan's best friend but their friendship was founded on innocence. They'd never had anything to test it, to measure their loyalty by; your dad having an affair wasn't the sort of thing either of them wanted to be dealing with. So instead, Ryan said he thought he was coming down with something and couldn't drink so there wasn't much point in going. Graham sympathized; he couldn't comprehend a non-alcoholic trip to the pub. Putting the phone down, Ryan welcomed silence like an old friend.

He opened a bottle of ouzo that his dad had brought back from Tenerife and decided to abuse it. Starting at eight in front of *EastEnders*, by the time the credits were rolling he couldn't focus properly. The channels took a few lolloping seconds to flip over; he thought he glimpsed pictures in between them and kept flicking; the programmes seemed trapped in the wooden frame of the TV screen. Turning it off brought the dimensions of the room into sharp relief, everything quiet with just the hush of cars sweeping down the road outside. Ryan put on an old Pixies record and knocked back the ouzo like he was Charlie Sheen in *Apocalypse Now*. He threw his fist at the screen of the old TV but drew back on the punch, ringing a pathetic knuckle rap on the glass. He hurled the cushions from the sofabed, laughing with someone else's laugh and sending the *Evening Mail* flying, pages falling like crippled birds over the carpet. A ringing in his ears became the phone and before he could reach it the answer machine had switched itself on.

'Ryan Brendle. If you want to leave a message – surprise surprise – leave it after the tone.'

– Ryan, returning the rather abrupt call of earlier, yer father.

As a child, Ryan had spent sick days in his father's car, riding in the leather front seat as his dad went from sale to sale. Listening to him pitch to clients over the phone he had heard a different man. That was the voice he heard now, the voice of his father's name: Ken Brendle.

– Stress at work or something? Call back if you get the message. I'll be on the carphone tomorrow, up until teatime.

Ryan went down on his knees and suddenly felt ready to puke, ouzo sugary in his mouth. He knelt over a page of the newspaper, trying to blink away the sickness and staring into the smiling face of a black boy. It was a school photo of the murdered boy on Hawes Lane and he tried reading the article to convince himself he was sober. After a few lines he staggered to the toilet. Before ten o'clock Ryan somehow managed to make the sofabed and crawled under the covers with Radio 4, trying to breathe in time with his violent stomach.

When he woke in the night, a World Service programme was reporting the plight of Chechnyan families searching for the disappeared.

Darren called. The clock by his bed said 12.00. He listened to Darren's voice and the noise of the store behind him, the clumsy racking of tills. Darren was asking him unanswerable questions and Ryan put the phone down. It rang again and he let it ring on as he climbed out of bed in yesterday's clothes and searched the room for his bus pass and *A–Z*. The pass turned up in the back pocket of his vomit-spotted jeans.

It began to drizzle as he pounded the suburban pavements of Weoley Castle. Ryan no longer felt the romantic and disaffected drunk; one night and one bottle of ouzo did not make you a glamorous depressive or an interesting psychological case, it just made your bones ache. His mother had always told him not to dwell on things. He wasn't even sure whether it was raining, the air was just wet. He sought evidence on the windscreens of cars, writing swearwords in the condensation and turning quickly from the streets, the finger-painted cars behind him. This made him feel petulant and childish, so he started drawing happy faces instead, flowers and suns.

Opposite the bus stop was a phone box and he had twelve minutes to make the call. He made it with four left.

– Ryan, yer father's been trying to call you.

– I've been trying to call him.

– And work phoned, they said yer off sick but haven't phoned up to tell them. Ryan, yer should say somethin' to 'em, love.

– I have, they're just incompetent.

– Oh Ryan, why would they be phoning me if they were that incompetent? They sounded completely at the end of their tether with yer.

– Yes, well, you're not responsible for me, are you? I'm responsible for myself now.

– I don't know, you tell me.

– I am telling you.

– Fine.

– Good.

There was a silence between them. He heard the kettle rise to a whistle, and pictured the kitchen, his mother cleaning up after herself as she made a sandwich and soup for lunch. *Neighbours* would be on the TV.

– Well, what is it, is there a message for yer dad?

– Not really.

– Not even going to send your love?

– No.

– Oh, charming. He said you were in a right mood. Are you ill?

– Yes.

– Well, what's wrong with yer?

– Think I've got flu. I've been sick.

– What, physically sick sick or just sick?

Ryan's voice began to go. – No, physically sick.

– Well, you don't get physically sick with the flu. Are you sure it's not a spot of food poisoning?

– Maybe, I don't eat well. He ground his teeth together and pinched his nose at the tears.

– Have you got a runny nose as well?

– Yeah.

– Well, you better get to bed. And phone work, all right?

Ryan had worked out where the church was, up in Blackheath, not far from work and one of the highest points in the Black Country. Council blocks climbed the hills where they could; the redbrick terraces ended abruptly on scrubland or gave way to trading estates. Some of these hills were hollowed by coal mining. He remembered a tale his grandad had told him about the great black caverns inside and thought of the bus's tyres treading the thin crust. The double-decker bullied its way through fall-out traffic from Merry Hill and he sat on the top deck, trying not to look down the driver's periscope. The day's *Evening Mail* carried more on its murder victim.

Andrew Collinmore had been sixteen, third-generation West Indian and born in Dudley. His mother described him as a bright child, in all the top sets except English, but a bit of a loner. He certainly hadn't been the kind to fall in with any gangs. He was taking nightclasses on top of school work; they kept him out of trouble. He had never been wayward at school except once – running down the corridor and knocking another boy over. He'd socialized mainly with girls and left behind a sweetheart who was devastated. They could see no reason why he should have been killed. Andrew hadn't been acting strangely at all. On the contrary, he'd been looking forward to his first visit to Jamaica that summer with his dad.

A picture of his parents at a TV appeal had them seated at a table with microphones clustering in on them; boom rods, cameras, journalists standing on their toes holding spotlights. Next to that another shot of Andrew, this time out of school uniform, posed by a home computer, hands held like a thunderbird puppet over the keys, smile strained. Ryan imagined the caption in a family album: Andrew's new computer.

He put the paper down and opened up the *A–Z*. There was no one left on the top deck. It smelled of stale cigarette smoke. As the bus whined on in first gear, Ryan watched cars circling a mini-roundabout on the hilltop. They were sliced from his view as they dropped down the other side. The bus followed, into a dell littered with boarded up shops on an abandoned estate. There was a real rain now, falling in dumb, unsatisfactory drops against the scratched Plexiglas windows of the bus, then working into a drumming of fingertips on the tin roof. Heavy clouds had turned the air a scorched-metal blue. As they climbed towards Hawes Lane, Ryan followed the pale yellow road of the *A–Z* until he reached a small cross. The bus slowed with a squeal of wet brakes.

Ryan sheltered in the bus stand on Hawes Lane and watched car headlights shovel through the downpour. The rain spat on the Cellophaned bundles of flowers that leaned into the corners of the shelter and darkened the toes of his trainers.

Andrew had a good last view from here, Ryan thought. At night the Black Country was a circuit of electric lights coiling over the hills, threads of roads and yellow streaks of motorways, the Merry Hill Centre just a soft glow on low clouds.

Ryan watched the flat grey concrete of the pavement coming alive in the rain.

Oxtail Soup

Sarah Martin

The colours blur and mingle into one, the music pumps on without stopping, stealing his mind. Air blasts at him from every direction, taking his breath away, making the hairs across the back of his neck rigid, his top dark with clammy sweat. It's all building up now, like an animal out of control, ready to swallow him whole, and the bass finally kicks in, his foot goes down harder; still the colours keep coming, faster and faster at him until he's in a tunnel of blur. It's like another world, and he closes his eyes for a second to escape the onslaught; objects are no longer objects, they're all just big shapes with no outlines. He can't take everything in, water keeps spilling from his eyes and the rush of air won't let them blink. He knows he has to focus on one thing, to prove to himself that he's still there. If he could keep his eyes open long enough without them stinging so much, he would look at that tree. That's what he would focus on if he weren't racing towards it, alone in his dad's Sierra, his eyes now firmly shut.

That's how it seemed to me anyway; there are still bits of it I wish I could remember better. Like the actual crash, I'd like to remember what that looked like. But now it's another new day, and Mum says I shouldn't think about it, that we should all forget about it, that I'm lucky to be alive. She always says the lucky-to-be-alive bit as if she's gasping for breath, and I can hear her at the door now, knocking just loud enough to let me know I should be awake, but not loud enough to actually wake me. A new day; rays of light are creeping in between my Formula One curtains, making weird patterns on the horrid carpet. Her head appears round the door along with a block of brightness, and in the half darkness I can just make out that she's wearing those slippers, the ones Dad says are bloody stupid; he reckons they'll make her fall down the stairs one day. And I can't look at the slippers – at her – so I roll over as if I'm just coming to, as if I've reached the stage when you know that you're awake but your hands are still all floppy. Actually I've been awake since 3.52. Wallace and Gromit live on the bedside table; they always make sure I know what time it is.

'Brian . . . Brian darling, it's eight o'clock.' Mum's voice is like her knock, quiet; her lips are probably pursed, and I feel like shouting *So?* at her, because it's never actually been agreed that eight o'clock is Brian-getting-up-time. But I don't shout, obviously.

'It's Wednesday morning –' she pauses, knowing I'll know the next bit '– so I've brought you Weetabix.' It's back to that then; Tuesdays we'd get tuna sandwiches in our packed lunches, Mondays we'd have macaroni cheese for tea. Mum's food-that-starts-with-the-letter-of-the-day game. Now I wonder if it's the only way she knows what day it is at all.

'I'll leave it here for you, all right? On your desk. Eat it quick or it'll go soggy . . .' She pulls the door shut quietly behind her.

I lift my head slowly in the darkness but everything feels all fat and woozy – I think I must be hot – so I sink my head back into the pillow, just catching the mumbled 'Elaines' and 'Dereks' outside on the landing. I stretch my legs out in the bed to starfish position so that my feet can find a cold bit, but there isn't one. The whole bed is baking and smelly, and as I try to stretch out a bit further, I realize I must have done it again. Mum's tucked me back in after finding me in some corner of the house, scared that I'd break out and that Mrs Perkins from number 32 would see me wandering round the front lawn, butt-naked. What Mrs Perkins would be doing watching our lawn at one a.m. is beyond me, but I don't bother asking.

The door to my room swings open without a knock, so I know it's him. He drags the curtains apart, making them flap on to my half-buried face. The light is painful, so I lug my heavy head over to face the open door where she's standing in the slippers. It's hard to say which side is worse.

'Brian . . .' He pauses, waiting for a reply. I can't ignore him. 'Mm?' is all he's going to get. 'Brian,' he says, louder now, 'get up.' And that's it, that's all he has to say. He leaves my room – bang – and I flinch. More 'Elaines' and 'Dereks', as he paces downstairs, the slippers slapping after him, stumbling slightly at the bottom. Front door slams, car revs up – not the Sierra, the courtesy one – tyres rip the gravel; silence.

Now it's quiet I can look around the room. I can't remember how long I've spent in here, but there are still new things to look at every day, and I like to save them for this time, a sort of treat every morning at Brian-getting-up-time. It's not my room, and because it used to be Barry's I can't change anything. They needed my room for the new office. So I've still got the Barry thing in here, matching stripy car curtains and duvet, Grandstand wallpaper with Des Lynam bits that used to give me nightmares, Matchbox red Ferraris all along the windowsill. Barry never used to let me play with them, not even the crappy ones with doors that didn't open and wheels that wouldn't go round. And so I've allowed myself the cars this morning. I've been building up to these for a while now. I never normally touch his stuff, but the cars are different, shiny as toffee apples, and my hand stretches out. The one by the pillow is the best; Barry must have wanted it close to him. I try to think what he used to do with them. All I remember is him begging for them – birthdays, Christmas – but he never used to play with them. I think he just liked to own them, and look at them sometimes. That was all he wanted them for.

Sometimes he would give me things though. He had this baseball cap that he wore all the time, and Dad would cough and Mum would say, 'Take your cap off at the table, Barry love,' and he would, but then he'd wink at me and wear it on his knee for the rest of tea. He gave me that cap, stinking of sweat and hair wax. 'Do you want this?' he said one day. 'I'm chucking it out, so you can have it, I s'pose . . . if you like.' I had to poke new holes in the plastic bit so it would fit my head properly, but I did want it and he knew it. Just like I knew he was never going to throw it out.

Sometimes we'd do stuff together too. I'd get home and Barry would come in a bit later because he'd had to walk from the other school, and we'd play games that he made up. When we were building our extension like the Perkins, the foundations were all dug out next to the house. Me and Barry would run inside them trying to hit each other as hard as we could with a manky old tennis ball. He always won. He'd stand on the ground looking down at me trying to hide in the tunnels, and he'd call my name and I'd know that I'd lost and that he'd cheated. I'd look up, blinking into the sun behind him, and it wouldn't matter that I'd lost because he'd be grinning, ready to get me with the ball at any minute. And then I'd remember it was a Friday – which meant something fried for tea – and Barry's girlfriend would be round later to sit with him in his room, in this room, listening to records, and I'd be sent up every ten minutes to check the door was still open. It always was.

I don't think I want to touch the cars any more. I'll look a little while longer and then decide what's next. There's not much left now apart from his clothes, and I'm going to leave those till last anyway. I sit up enough to look closely at the last car on the sill, and my eyes are just over the window-ledge, so that I can see everything. No one can see me. Not unless they're really looking and I like that. I can see myself in the window too: my hair's gone all spiky with grease and I've got crusty sleep all over my face. But no one can see. So it doesn't matter, does it?

The sky is dead blue, really dark like at the beach, but I don't want to feel that heat, the hazy type of high summer heat that you have to fight for breath in. That gives you sweat patches as soon as you open the door. The heat in here is always the same; Dad sets it on the thermostat near the front door.

The sky slopes down on to the rows of houses, all with satellite dishes and security lights, and then slides past droopy hanging baskets into front gardens with yellowy dry patches and bird feeders. I can see hundreds from here, hundreds of bird feeders and houses of Elaines and Dereks and Barrys and Brians, because our house is right opposite the three new roads – Crafts Way, Kirkby Close and Ray-smith Avenue, that last one named after a binman. It really pissed Mum and Dad off; he thought it would lower the price of houses and Mum agreed. Me and Barry just thought it was a shitty name for a road, and that it was funny that no one knew how to say it – 'Ray Smith' like the actual name, or 'racemith' if you wanted it to sound posh.

The big cars have gone from outside all the houses – so the Dereks must have gone to work. Most of the Elaines have their own cars too, even if not all of them go anywhere. Mum doesn't really like driving, not even to the Co-op, so we sold hers. We used to have a caravan too, dead big, but then we had to sell that as well. Dad told Mr Perkins we were 'trading it in for a better model', so at the minute we must still be looking.

I must have been staring out for a while, because it's the knock again. Lunch, which means it's 12.45, and Wallace agrees when I check. She bustles more this time, because the slippers have gone, traded in for black lace-ups and tan tights, and she puts down the Birds of Britain tray next to Wallace, and uncreases a crease that isn't really there from her apron.

'You didn't eat your Weetabix,' she says. *No shit Sherlock*, as Barry would have said. Her nose wrinkles up as if she's about to gag, and she sighs – louder than normal – and bustles over to the window. 'It's ever so stuffy in here you know . . . you need some fresh air. Why don't you go out for a while . . . Mm? Brian, I said why don't you go out for a while?'

I think she thinks I'm mad, or just thick, because she talks like I don't understand her. She opens the window as if to say that she knows that I won't go anywhere, but at least I could stop her house from smelling.

'I don't really want to,' I answer quietly.

Her whole face wrinkles, but she takes a breath and makes herself speak, voice spiky like cactus. 'Dad'll have to get round to that bird thingy one of these days . . . you'll be able to see all sorts then . . .' She trails off, uncreasing her apron again, her other hand drifting to her head and smoothing down a sticky-out bit of hair. She turns round then, looking straight at me, knowing she could never smooth down my spikes, and I can tell she's itching to wipe off my face crust with a licked finger, but she knows not to try.

I look away, down to the soup which even Gromit is turning his nose up at. 'It's oxtail. It'll make you feel better.' She's given up on the food game then – Wednesday always was the difficult one. She did really well once with Wieners, those hot dog sausages that you can just about eat by sucking, but

Dad said he didn't like them. 'Don't you think they're bland, boys? I think they're bland, Elaine,' he said, and so we only had proper sausages after that.

She's facing the window now, nicer than facing me, I guess, and the voice is back to cactus. 'We've had a letter from the farmer . . . he's not going to press charges, given the circumstances –' she trails off again '– which is lucky really, isn't it? It means we've only got to think about the police, which is lucky . . .' And then it's back to safe soup. 'I thought you used to like oxtail,' she says to the window, puzzled.

'That was Barry,' I say to the soup. 'I like chicken.'

There's no reply to that. She closes the window, turns, hands me the soup, picks up the Birds of Britain tray and leaves the room. Through the banisters, I can't see her head going down the stairs, so she must be just there, behind my doorway, back to the landing wall, tray shaking in front of her. She doesn't think I've ever seen her, but I have, loads of times. Not at first, I didn't see her for ages, and then I'd walk past and she'd be in a room, shaking, or we'd be at dinner, and she'd say, 'Excuse me a moment,' as if me and Dad were the Queen, and I'd be able to hear her from the downstairs loo in the extension, but I'd never say anything when she came back in time for tinned peaches. I'd just ask to be excused.

The head goes down the stairs now, and I look at the soup, thick and brown – almost black – and the smell makes me retch, because oxtail *was* his favourite. I wasn't lying. His soup went cold that night; your food always went cold if you weren't at the table at six. It was just the way it worked, and it didn't make sense that he wasn't there, cap on his knee, guzzling down the beefy stock while I dunked chunks of bread roll in mine to try and soak it up so it would look like I'd eaten it all. It didn't make sense that there was a phone call at dinnertime – everyone knew not to phone the Taylor house at six, it was a running joke. None of it made sense; the special assembly where no one would look at me, everyone saying it was such a shame and so unexpected, because even Dad had said that Barry was good at driving.

Giving us soup on Barry's birthday. Oxtail soup. Shitty brown shitty thick oxtail soup. It wasn't even a Saturday or Sunday; there was no reason to have soup at all, let alone oxtail. Especially that day, when in other years we'd have shared parties, goodie bags with clowns on the front and sweets inside, the flying saucer ones you pop with your tongue to get the sherbet out first. Wrapped-up chunks of cake with jam in that always got stuck to the serviette. On that night Barry should have had a cake with candles and a car on, and he would have blown out all the candles first time. But there was only oxtail soup, that smell of beef bones and dried blood, and when I came downstairs and saw it I dreaded us sitting there going through the motions. Dad asking for the salt, and her getting offended but passing it anyway; me pretending to like the soup and trying to forget that opposite me, where there should have been a cake, there was only an empty chair and one of those shiny green mats with a picture of the countryside on.

But it was worse than that. Dad didn't even ask for the salt, and Mum just seemed relieved that no one had mentioned anything. And then after the soup had gone, after I'd forced down as much as I could without it making me lose everything over the countryside mats, she asked me what she asks me every time, 'So how was school today?' I knew I couldn't answer – the soup had clogged me up – and if I tried to talk I'd end up spewing beefy oxtail bubbles all over the rose dining room. And then Dad chipped in too. 'Brian, your mother asked you a question,' and of course I knew that she had, and that he'd said something too, but the soup had got into my ears – all I could hear was gloop. How could

I say I was clogged up? How could I explain about Mr Hill saying it was a shame I wasn't more like Barry, and then blushing? And the girl in my form who said Brian was a crap name, that it made me sound like a gimp, and me wishing I'd been called something like 'Nick' anyway, because 'Nick Taylor' sounds like someone who'd be good at rugby, who would know how to have a laugh. And about how this was all there was – oxtail soup, and the Perkins, and Kirkby Close – and that I could tell I'd be here for ever, that I was here and he wasn't, and that no one had seemed to notice the difference anyway. I knew that if I just said 'Fine' like always, I'd only be adding to it all; and the whole house would become covered with gloopy oxtail, glooping up all the doors and windows, filling up the rose dining room, and her slippers, and his Matchbox cars. So I just got up.

I stood up; got up without being excused first, and walked past Dad at the end of the table, past the family photos, past the thermostat and out of the front door. It made sense at the time to pick up the keys from the key bowl next to the phone on my way out. She wanted to follow me apparently, but he stopped her. I bet it was, 'Elaine, leave him. He'll get hungry and come in in a bit,' and then, 'Yes, I suppose you're right.' Both of them sitting there at their seats, waiting to drown in brown gloop while I was unlocking the front door to the Sierra. He didn't know I'd taken the car keys, if he had it would have been, 'For God's sake woman, stop him. He can't take the car!' and then, 'Yes, I suppose you're right.' But he didn't see, so he didn't have to be worried about me or the car, and they probably both sat there, finishing their dinner, Mum sighing and saying, 'I'll heat it up for him later. He won't be long I bet.' Both of them turning to soup.

I had to pull the seat right forward, as far as it'd go, to reach the pedals, and I tried to remember everything Barry had said when he was learning, about the clutch and everything. The car jumped forward when I turned the key, and as I ground the stick into reverse and hopped off the driveway I wasn't really thinking about where I'd go, just that I *had* something – that right then, at that moment, I was owning his car. It was harder than I thought, and it took me loads of stalls before I could get going and get the windows and the sunroof open and the stereo on. And so there I was, making a circuit of Kirkby Close and Crafts Way, trying to keep my hand on the wheel and pull down the sunguard thing at the same time, and I knew if I could turn out at the end I'd be on the Redditch Road, and then there'd be no stopping me because that road was straight and went on for ever. I was probably only going about fifteen miles an hour when I got to the end of the road, but it felt faster being at the wheel, and I turned right without checking, without waiting for Mum to say 'Safe this way' like she always did with Dad.

The road was thin at first until I got past all the Elaine and Derek houses, and it was only when the road got wider that I wondered where I was going, and the truth was I wasn't going anywhere in particular. I twiddled with the stereo till it went so loud it made the speakers fuzz, and I opened all the windows with the buttons that me and Barry always fiddled with, that Dad told us off for, and pushed my foot down as far as it would go, waiting every time till I could hear the engine above the stereo before pulling or pushing the gearstick. And then everything went a bit funny – colours blurring, music pumping – but I knew that at least I wasn't going to be clogged, that the soup couldn't gloop me at this speed. That was all I was bothered about, it didn't really matter if I was watching where I was going or not.

When they got to me I could tell they were worried, because the doctor looked at them a bit funny; Dad still had gravy in his moustache from dinner, and normally Mum would have told him to wipe it off before they came out of the dining room, let alone the house.

And another new day's nearly over. I can see him now when I look down, his bald head is there through the sunroof of the car which has just turned on to the driveway. All the Dereks are coming home now. That means it's only quarter of an hour before the Birds of Britain'll be back again, to join the Weetabix and the oxtail soup, and I can feel it all clogging together. At least the smell's gone – without the beef bone smell it looks like it could be chocolate sauce, or a bowl of gravy, and all I can smell now is me. Sweaty duvets and greasy hair, and morning breath even though it's six o'clock, and face crust, and it's like I'm glooping up myself, instead of waiting for the soup to do it for me. And I don't want her nose to wrinkle or his moustache to twitch when they walk in the room to leave the tray any more, and I don't want to be a Derek, getting home in time for tea, eating food that matches the day, never saying, well, anything. Never even saying his name.

And I know I have to open the window and so I do, moving the Ferraris round while I swing open the wood and let roasted air hit me in my face, and it's not like I thought it'd be. The sun's still there, making the dry patches more yellow with the heat and the hanging baskets droopier but it's not the hazy type I thought it'd be, it's less sweaty. There's a bit of a breeze, kind of sharp on my face, brushing through my spikes, drying the sweat, and I want to shout his name. But I don't shout, obviously.

Wrecked

Neil Hall

Drinking alone has never been entertaining; being drunk alone is. Any connoisseur of happy hours can tell you that. Caught somewhere between the Crown's dim half-light and the stained wallpaper, anonymity is guaranteed, forming a whole new perspective from which to view reality. The 'define me' nature of Broad Street's larger bars is too conspicuous for my purposes. People come and go, you and the drink remain. Always the drink. The finest clientele Stephenson Tower has to offer mixing freely with unabashed businessmen fumbling their attempts to seduce their secretaries. Shameless couples, tramps wisely investing the profits of their begging. Shifty characters steadying their nerves after visits to the Sunset cinema, the excitement too much for them to contain. All are united by the same passion, the chance to find a hole or space in the world where you don't exist any more. To not exist has always been easier – though admittedly harder to achieve – than existing. The booze erodes the barriers between the two extremes. The tragic and depressive unite to become comic and impressive.

*

The motorway service station coffee does nothing to revive my spirits. It tastes of chewy cigarette ends – the whisky miniature I bought myself is too precious to waste in coffee like this. I down it immediately to swill the taste from my mouth. The restaurant is pretty much empty, my only companions the teenagers desperate to avoid the family do and chuffed to be on triple time. Their hangovers do nothing for their complexions or, for that matter, their skills in customer relations. It can't get any worse. Can it?

I soon realize that when I'm reduced to thinking in crap clichés about the standard of my life that it probably can't. But the 'realizing' somehow makes it worse; I'm not just desperate, I *know* that I am and there must be millions of desperate people in the world better off than me just because they don't realize it. Lucky bastards.

I head back to my car. It's one of those things I've been meaning to change, just never got round to. A healthy slap of mud covers the beginnings of rust around the wheel arches. A dent in the boot: I didn't see the tree until I hit it. As I pull out of the car park and back on to the motorway my senses are assaulted by the garish decor of Tamworth service station. It's been up since November. It's knackered. A fitting symbol for the anticlimax that is Christmas.

The badly wrapped present beside me is for my dad. It is the only present I had to buy this year and is squatting among the empty soft drink and fast food packaging. The motorway is hardly busy: everyone else is probably at home wearing matching jumpers, kissing under mistletoe or building Lego islands. Unable to face the cheesy Radio 1 Christmas, I root for a tape among the discarded boxes that lie in the recess in front of the gearstick. The first that comes to hand is an old one, *Achtung Baby*. I've not heard it for ages; it was a sixth form thing.

Karen never did like U2. She didn't get it. Bono's crooning pissed her off, especially in the car.

'I still don't get why I have to drive anyway.'

'Look, Jane and Christopher are mostly my friends and I'd like a drink with them tonight, all right? You can still have a couple and chat about your football or something.'

'But you don't even like drinking, and as for Christopher, he doesn't know the first thing about –'

'Don't start. He's a perfectly nice bloke. It's not as if I'm asking you to spend the whole day with my dad or anything –'

'But –'

'No! There are no buts. Or shall I bring up the "incident". That little episode of yours . . .'

She was always doing that. Bringing up the 'incident', as she called it, without actually bringing it up. Resigned to the fact that I was going to have to spend the evening talking to boring Christopher, I figured a gesture of smug defiance was the least I could do.

'Driver always gets choice of music, you know that, it's your rule.' I put my tape in and received an unimpressed frown for my troubles.

'What's so good about a middle-aged man in tight leather trousers, cowboy boots and naff sunglasses anyway?'

'It's Bono,' I plead, mentally singing along.

'I don't care. The only reason he sings like that is 'cos of those ridiculous too-tight trousers.'

'But it's Bono. His name means "good" for "good voice" in Latin or Italian or something.'

'I think he's taking the piss. Dressing up like that and then singing as though he's trying to communicate with whales or something. He's either taking the piss or he's gay.' She screwed her nose up, her triumphant I've-made-a-good-point gesture.

'It's Bono, he can't be gay.'

'What do you mean he can't be gay? What sort of a remark is that?' She did that cute slack-jawed, disgusted-eyebrow thing.

'Look, everyone knows there are certain people that just aren't gay. Bono's one of them and Vinnie Jones and then there's that bloke whatsisname, from *Die Hard*, Bruce Willis. Now c'mon, they are never gay.'

'Oh and who is then?'

'Well, er . . . I dunno. There's that bloke from REM, he's got to be gay now, hasn't he? I mean, come on –'

'And you talk about *women's* logic. You do realize there's not one ounce of sense in anything you've just said.'

'But there is –'

'Not a single ounce, and you're supposed to be intelligent. God only knows what the rest of your primeval mates are like.'

'Like me with less big words.'

'That's right, do what you always do, resort to your pathetic little smart-arse comments. Honestly, I don't know why I . . .'

She began to lecture and simultaneously fiddle fastidiously with an already tidy glove compartment.

It was at this point I turned the stereo up. The not-so-adult equivalent of shoving your fingers in your ears and shouting 'Ner-nuh-ne-ner-ner, I can't hear you.' As in childhood, it didn't work.

'You're just bloody impossible. It's not as though you're content to taunt me with his voice though, is it? You have to bloody sing along and you know you can't sing, so you just shout loudly and tunelessly, your very own form of torture.'

'*Who's* gonna *ride* your *wild horses*? *Who's* gonna *fall* at the foot of *thee*?'

'I still haven't forgiven you yet, you know. I'll never forget that karaoke at my mum's fiftieth. God, you can be so cringeworthy.'

The slightest hint of a smile cracked through Karen's stern demeanour. Finally my willingness to humiliate myself in public had paid dividends. She never could stay mad at me for long. Not then, anyway.

She never was mad at me really. Not really really anyhow – she just left. I don't think I did that much wrong, just nothing much particularly right.

'You're just so ooomphwarr,' she used to say.

I used to think that it made me sound quite cool, you know, all mysterious and enigmatic, so much so that she didn't know how best to describe me, a challenge. But then the accompanying arm gestures got bigger and tighter. The hands clenched. The smile that used to follow waited and waited and then didn't come any more. Neither did she.

It's ten a.m. This time last Christmas I was being treated to a session of private modelling of the black lacy underwear I bought her from Ann Summers. I may not have admitted it then, and she may not believe me now, but that wasn't the 'thing' – the sex was only part of it. I'd swap it all for one glimpse of that look in her eye she used to get. I'd walk into the bar, room or restaurant and her eyes would scream 'I love you!' from up to thirty yards away. Of course I'd smile coyly, too cool to notice or let on that I knew, but I did and I always will. One time I made her so happy she cried. How can I ever better that? I wanted to piss my name in the snow in July for her. I couldn't do that either.

The car's heater breathes down my neck and tingles my spine.

Now she's with fucking Marcus. In fact she's probably fucking fucking Marcus right now. Modelling the saucy underwear he bought her, the pervert, or worse still, wearing the stuff I got her last year 'cos Marcus didn't buy any. Twat.

I'm going home – just me, my dad and 'pass us the salt, son' conversation. Merry Christmas. I lean across to the passenger seat and grab his present. The paper tears easily. I got him a bottle, same as always, except this time I begin to drink it. There seems little point in waiting to swap a Glenfiddich for a Jamesons; it makes no difference to me and I'm in need of a little Christmas cheer.

When driving on the motorway, reality is a useful concept; one which brings a temporary halt to my drinking. The monotony of the scenery is excruciating – tree, embankment, hedge, cow, tree, embankment. My eyes fix upon a hedge a little too long, the car lurches to the right, my stomach lurches to the left, my head attempts both and achieves neither. I regain control and drink just a little more.

Last time I went home for Christmas, East 17 were number one but no one liked them. Twelve-year-old girls have a lot to answer for. That was just after my first term at uni. Dad had picked me up from the train station, just me and him on Christmas day, like now. That was the last time I spoke to any of my mates from home. Nice as they are, types of car, the working of engines and gossip about people I went to school with are not interesting. The worst of the lot, though, has to be when they try to talk to me about something they think I will be interested in, that they actually haven't got a clue about. I mentally and physically have to bite my tongue. It doesn't matter that the word ignoramus is visible in my eyes. Football, beer and birds can only get you so far, and often it's not far enough.

Eleven o'clock, Christmas Eve, just before closing it was, we all left the Bell Inn. We wandered down across the square, the usual kebab versus club debate raging – which is better, pubs or clubs? The rain tried its best to dampen our inebriated festivities. All around us blokes in loud shirts were having the exact same argument; the more canny ones watched which direction the fit birds were walking. Reeking of Malibu and Archers, wearing too short skirts and too high heels, a group of tinsel-clad slappers walked by.

'Phwooar, ay, not bad are they, lads? I'd do 'er. That fit

one. Did ya see 'er wink at me? She wants it, and she's gonna get it all right. C'mon lads, I'll let you share 'er mates out – it's Christmas after all.'

'You're all fuckin' heart, aren't ya, Dave! It was me she was looking at, you ugly fucker! Just for that you can 'ave the sad ugly mate.'

You know, they say a great aptitude for the game of pool is the sign of a misspent youth. They are wrong. A faultless knowledge of the ingredients of cocktails and first-hand experience of petty crime, mind-altering drugs and sexually transmitted diseases are far greater signs. I'm fucking shit at pool.

For years before that my dad and anyone else with an opinion kept telling me I was in with the wrong crowd. Course I didn't fucking listen, I never did. Too cocksure of myself, I needed to work it out. Took me a while though, several scrapes and near misses. Got caught once though, let off with a caution.

'I'm sorry. It won't happen again, honest. I've learnt my lesson.'

Silence.

'It was Craig's fault. You're right, he's a bad influence.'

No reply.

'OK. OK. It was stupid. I was stupid. I should've . . .'

A large hand gripped me on the shoulder.

'. . . I should've listened to you.'

I was shoved towards our car. He looked at me a while, stared down at me, the rage in his eyes talking for him.

'I'm sorry. I'll grow up. I'll try harder. I, I, I won't let you down again . . .'

Still nothing. Not even a guilt trip.

'Sorry . . .' I mumbled.

The rage eventually gave way to disappointment or shame,

and then rage returned more fierce than before. He just looked and when I dared I looked back.

'Your dad's gay!' she said. It was one of those post-sex, frolicking in bed, 'Yeah, well, I've shagged your mum' conversations.

'Don't be gross.'

'He is, face it.'

We both stared at the pastel-coloured ceiling.

'He can't be gay. He's my dad for God's sake.'

'Why does that mean he can't be gay?'

'I dunno, well, he's from Yorkshire, isn't he? Where men are men and poofs are beaten.'

'Yeah, well he's not had a woman in his life for over, er, how long is it now?'

'Fourteen years, since Mum . . .'

I roll away from her, taking the yellow and blue duvet with me.

'He spends all his time with his best mate Les –'

'So. You've got to have friends. He's retired, he needs hobbies and mates and stuff.'

'He spends all his time going out with someone called Leslie, who's not a woman . . .'

The argument became more and more tenuous.

'Shut it and come 'ere, you.'

I tickled her. She hated that.

The joy that the bottle is still half full warms my throat; the despair that it is simultaneously nearly empty hurts my head. The crisp sunlight provides a nauseating warmth through the car windscreen. My stomach growls. My hands shake. I grip hard and firm on the wheel. The shaking from my hands dances a conga down my arm before trampolining inside my head. I retch, not enough to make me sick, just enough for the taste of whisky to fill my mouth and tease me into drinking more. It's cunning like that, really fucking cunning.

'The biggest mistake they made was letting Deano go. To get out of this division you need firepower, a touch of quality, class. Selling 'im 'as clearly reduced our goals per game ratio.'

'Oh yeah, well, I suppose . . .'

Since his retirement my dad had become a disciple of Andy, a real Sky Sports junkie, eager for his fix of mind-numbing statistics and multi-perspective replays.

'We didn't even get much money for 'im. I know 'e was old, but where are we gonna get a replacement of 'is quality? . . . Exactly. We can't, we won't. Serious lack of ambition, always 'as been.'

Don't get me wrong, I like football, it's just that since his retirement my dad and his mate Les have immersed themselves in the Sheffield United supporters' association to an unhealthy degree. They were now mixing with – and on a par with – the sort of people who know every player's birthday, inside leg measurements and children's names. Treading that fine line between supporters and stalkers.

'You're coming for Christmas then?'

'Well, yeah, if it's all right.'

'Great. I'll get a turkey. You'll stay for Boxing Day, won't you? West Brom at home, real biggie. Marcello might be back from injury, you've got to see 'im play, he's true quality. Come for a few drinks with me and Les. We'll update you on what's what, eh? Tell you who to watch for an' that. They're not a bad side, West Brom either, you know . . .'

A walking Rothman's yearbook complete with obsessive tendencies.

Nearly there, one junction away. The lack of air in the car grasps my attention, the car's smaller, the motorway's busier. I wind my window down; it doesn't help. I turn on the blower; years' worth of dust blows in my face. My head throbs, the cars in front of me leave the road and draw a circle in the air. A burning sensation creeps up from my stomach to the back of my throat. My eyes shut. The car does a somersault. An exit approaches. I jerk the wheel and point the car in roughly the right direction. Straight on round the roundabout and into the nearby layby.

It's busy. A couple of cars and a Portakabin café. The smell of boiled onions and cheap burgers does not help my cause. I leg it to the hedgerow. Gasping for pure air. Gravel crunches. Too late. My stomach erupts. I chunder a blotch of red cornflakes and coffee on to the greenest hedge in Britain. The stench of whisky and bile does battle with the burgers and onions. There can be no victor. I'm sick again. A gloopy trail of red saliva leads from my mouth to the floor. I bat it away with my hand and drag it down my shirt. I lean back, hands on hips, staring in awe of the mess I've created.

'You should never touch 'er food, mate. 'Er coffee's just about safe, but the burgers are lethal.'

'Ugh' is all I manage in response.

'You OK? Look in a bit of a bad way, that's all.'

'Fine, fine, s'leave us alone.'

As the figure approaches he comes into focus.

'My life, son, you don't 'alf reek, eeeuugh, your sick –' he gestures towards the mess '– does that 'appen often? Oi Charlie, Charlie, get over 'ere now.'

A second figure approaches, bigger than before with harder edges.

'Awwwww, that's foul, bloody awful. We better take 'im in. Is that 'is vehicle too?'

'Yeah, I think I saw 'im ger' out.'

'Fuckin' Christmas Day too, and on me bloody coffee break. Do you think we enjoy nicking twats like you, son?'

'Take it easy, Charlie. 'E's in a bad way, look at 'im.'

'Bad way! He's steamin' – an 'e was driving. Well done, you talentless twat. Drank lots at a party, go 'n' kill someone in me car, very bloody clever –'

I'm bundled into the back of their car. I lie down and succumb to an overwhelming urge to sleep.

I can't remember if I was sitting or standing; sitting, probably. She was definitely standing, in that gap between the stereo and the television. I can't see her face, though. I want to, but I can't.

'. . . you spend all day publishing bloody fairy stories and then come home and act like a five-year-old and it's not on. When are you going to do something proper?'

'I do, I do. I publish literature for older children and teenagers, *not* fucking fairy tales, working at the third biggest –'

'Don't you give me your sales speech! I'm not on about that. Take some responsibility for a change, seize the day, for Christ's sake don't drift. Bloody do something –'

'Like what? What exactly do you want me to do?'

'Take an interest, form an opinion on something, break out of your tedious little comfort zone, participate in something for once, don't fuck things up completely, leave a mark –'

'Are you gettin' clucky? Is that what this is all about, 'cos you know my –'

'*No!* That's not it, that's not it at all, you just don't get it at all. You really don't know, do you? You just don't get it at all.'

'Get *what*?'

'*Enough*. Enough. That says it all. I'm going. Call me when you've thought about it.'

As usual, while I sleep, the conversation plays in my dream. That was it, just words, no pictures. Her words are scalded into my memory, my frantic brain searches for answers. The door slams in my head. The only image I can see is an empty space in my living room.

I shiver myself awake. Artificial fluorescent light stuns my eyes. I raise my head from the desk in front of me; the pool of drool remains. I'm in a room full of good advice: 'Join Neighbourhood Watch', 'Say NO to drugs', 'Kill your speed'. The wall's screams force me to put my head back on the table, drawing the police-issue blanket closer. The blanket darkens where it absorbs my sweat. My hands refuse to stop shaking.

Time passes. I still shake and sweat, a little less than before. I'm in a corridor now, a corridor that imitates a reception area. A man enters through a doorway and looks, just looks. He walks up to the desk and enquires about something. He stares down at me, rounder than before, and with a forced smile acknowledges my existence. I wearily raise myself to my feet. He reaches up to place an arm around my shoulder; then guides me to the car.

On the Rails

Nick Rendall

The dull grey light of another day coldly wakes the estate. The bottles and needles from the night before decorate the concrete courtyard. A burnt-out car sits blackened on its rims, evidence of another successful joyride. The future looks bleak for the people who live in the system-built estate. It is a place of boredom and hardship.

Billy's eyes opened slowly. He stared blankly at the wall for a minute, then rolled over and reached for his cigarettes. The packet was empty. This was distressing. He grumbled quietly to himself and began to make a roll-up from the nubs in the ashtray. Leaning out of his twelfth-floor window, he sparked his fake Zippo and lit the second-hand cigarette. It tasted more of ash than tobacco. The smoke looked pure white against the dreary greys which filled his view.

Billy got dressed and went into the kitchen to search for something edible.

'Have we got any food, Mum?' he yelled.

'You what?' He'd woken her up.

'Food. Is there any food?'

'In the cupboard. There's loads.'

'Food. Not crap,' Billy said quietly. He found some stale bread. There was a scraping of margarine in the tub, crunchy with crumbs. 'It's unhealthy to eat shit food all the time, you know. You can get rickets.'

'Stop bloody moaning,' his mother croaked.

Billy took a bite of his stale sandwich and tossed it in the bin. He looked for some money. The jar was empty except for three shiny pound coins, which he pocketed.

'Billy, go to school,' she said.

'Yeah, I'm going.'

Billy looked out of his window. His mates were kicking a football around, except Neil, who was working on their piece. Billy smiled. He grabbed his spray cans and put them in his bag. He called goodbye to his mother as he walked out the door. He ran downstairs and out into the courtyard.

'All right, Neil.'

'Morning, Billy.'

'Starting early then?'

'I reckon we can have it finished by the end of the morning.'

Their piece was quite large – about six metres across and three metres high. They'd started spraying a week ago. The picture was an imaginary landscape of jagged ochre cliffs, distant violet mountains, a fiery sky. The clouds formed a ferocious yellow-eyed animal baring its teeth over the scene. There was just a small corner left to spray.

After a couple of hours the piece was complete. They signed their names underneath and stepped back to admire what they had done. It looked amazing against the dirty greys of the estate.

'We'll make sure nobody paints over this one, Billy.'

'Yeah. This one stays. Who got the car?'

'My brother,' Neil said proudly. 'BMW 325i, the ultimate

driving machine. He took it to a hundred an' ten on the High Street.'

'My brother died on a joyride. Hit a concrete post,' Billy said with a bitter, cold voice.

There was silence for a few seconds, but it seemed like an hour.

Then Neil broke it. 'At least he died happy.'

Billy laughed.

A group of five or six boys came over from where they had been playing football.

'Nice piece,' Kevin said. 'Wanna come down the track?'

Billy and Neil looked at each other and grinned. They all set off across the car park, Billy and Neil walking behind the others.

'I've got a spliff from last night,' Neil said, reaching into his pocket. He put it into his mouth, lit it and took a few puffs. 'When did your brother die then?' he asked, as he passed the joint to Billy.

'Ta. Before we moved here. We used to live with my dad, see, but he went off with some bimbo. My brother was really mad. He nicked a car and the pigs chased him into a post. He died quick, though. Me and my mum moved here after that.'

They came to the wire fence which surrounded the car park. One by one they climbed through the hole and down a steep slope thick with brambles to the railway track. There was a signal tower with a ladder leading up to a large platform. Originally grey, it was now a mass of fading graffiti as everyone in the area had put their tag on it. They all climbed to the top and sat on the railing running round the edge of the platform. The youngest kid there, Darren, pulled out a paper bag, put it to his face and inhaled deeply. He passed it to the next boy who did the same. Glue was the cheapest way to get high. Where they lived everybody wanted to get high; there was nothing else to do.

'TRAIN!' someone shouted.

They were on their feet and climbing down the ladder in a moment. This was a regular pastime so they were quick to take up their positions. Darren stayed on the tower to judge the winner.

Now they were all on the track except Darren. The train emerged from a tunnel about a mile down the line.

'Who's gonna beat Neil, then, lads?' Darren yelled from his perch.

Neil was always the last to move. He would stand there looking totally relaxed and then with about three metres between him and the train he would dive off the track and get up smiling. It was as if he had no fear. He had somehow lost the instinct for self-preservation.

Billy's heart was beating hard and fast. He looked at Neil, who winked. Billy concentrated on the train. It was about three-quarters of a mile away and closing fast. And then the effect of the glue hit him. His heart started beating normally again. His eyes could see the train bearing down on him but his brain didn't register. He stared blankly as if he was looking into space. The train was about twenty metres away, the driver leaning on his whistle. Everyone jumped off the track but Billy. He just stood there. Calm and relaxed. The train seemed to be moving in slow motion. Then he felt his heart stop. There was a noise like an explosion. Everything was black. The noise got quieter and quieter and eventually faded away.

It's drizzling. The sky is that same dull grey again. Neil is standing gazing at the piece he did with Billy. He takes a sprayer from his bag and begins some lettering above the piece. A few minutes later he hears a car pull up. He turns round ready to run but sees it's a taxi. Billy's mother steps out dressed all in black. She wipes the tears from her eyes to read what Neil has been writing. She smiles. 'In Memory of Billy O'Donnell'. Neil nods at her and she does the same. There is no need to speak.

Hard Shoulder

Julia Bell

I suppose what I liked best about living round there was the roads. The wide liquorice strips of concrete and tar that snaked around the city, the long, tree-lined dual carriageways, the bottleneck A-roads, the six-way roundabouts, the ski-jump flyovers, the Smartie-tube tunnels, the Spaghetti Junction.

Most folk hated it, all the traffic and pollution. Mum always looked down her nose like she'd trodden in something nasty when she came to visit.

– Not good for you, you know, she'd say, lighting the tip of another Silk Cut Ultra. – All that carbon monoxide, give you cancer like your nan.

She always looked at me as if she couldn't quite figure me out any more. As if the distance between us was something that I'd chosen, not something that was forced between us by that bastard of a boyfriend of hers.

Strange, really. I always thought it would be me who left the flat when I was sixteen, not my mum.

Sometimes, when I looked out of the window down on to the estate, I could see what she hated so much. All the blocks lined up like Lego, bits chipped off, windows boarded up, flats smashed, squatted. The lumpy women with prams and squealing toddlers, their figures ruined by babies and Burger King. The swarms of boys huddling and squabbling in the stairwells. It's not what she'd call respectable.

I'll never forget how she looked when he first came round in his Ferrari. We stood on the balcony, looking down, as he pulled up to the car park at the bottom of the block.

– Oh Mandy, she said. – Will you look at the state of that. And she sighed like she'd just taken off a tight pair of shoes.

I watched them drive away after the wedding. The car did a slow circuit of the estate, Mum in the front with her sunglasses on, him gripping the wheel with his poncy leather driving gloves. I think she expected people to come out and wave. They slipped on to the road and were gone. Zooming off up the dual carriageway, just a blur of red then nothing.

It was weird for a while. No screeching telephone conversations, no thickets of bleached blond hair in the bathplug, no one telling me to do the hoovering. I lounged round the flat watching TV, eating Pot Noodles and crisps and not bothering to wash up. I was supposed to be going to college to get my certificates but I rang them and told them I was contagious and wasn't coming back. No one ever checked to see if it was true; they sent me letters that I never opened and left to pile up by the door.

I picked up some casual work at the Vauxhall. It was one of those sixties pubs; an extension of someone's front room, full of old blokes off the estate drinking their pensions or sick benefit. They went there because the bitter was a quid a pint and Billy turned a blind eye to their scams: cheap tobacco, the occasional crate of whisky. When he hired me, I told Billy I was twenty-one. I did weekdays and evenings at weekends. Mum would have had a fit if she'd found out, she still thought I was going to college. She wanted me to get my qualifications and go to university.

– It's the only way you'll ever get out of here, she said to me, unless you get a man.

I could tell by the way she said it she thought this was highly unlikely. She had told me before that I didn't wear the right kind of clothes to attract men. She thought I should be more upfront, wear shorter skirts and higher heels.

– You really don't make the best of yourself, Mandy, she would say, pausing to pick a stray hair from my top or straighten my collar. – It's a shame, you're not bad looking you know. I knew that really I disappointed her. She wanted a daughter like Sonya downstairs, born complete with lip liner and size five feet.

At the Vauxhall it didn't make a damn bit of difference what I wore. I would've got groped in a duffle coat. There was always some hand slithering, searching for an excuse to brush against my breasts or thighs. Trisha, Billy's wife, always wore jeans if she was downstairs.

– Can't be arsed with this lot, she used to say, grinning at me from her stool at the end of the bar. – Fancy anything on legs in here. No point in giving them any more reasons to perve.

I liked Trisha. She said she was thirty-two but it seemed hard to tell. She helped out sometimes at weekends when it got mad busy, but she would always make mistakes on the till. She was someone my mum would say was throwing herself away. She sat at the end of the bar drinking while I worked, gossiping about the customers, giving me tips on the racing, or telling me stories about when she lived in America and had the time of her life. She said she drove a '76 Chevy from New York to San Francisco all by herself.

One day, when Billy was off at the races and Trisha was in charge of the bar, she decided to make some cocktails.

– Let's get pissed, she said, let's get wasted. She jumped off the barstool and bustled behind the bar. She looked at the optics. – A Violator, she said, let's start with a Violator.

She shook up some vodka and Martini in the silver shaker. Then she filled two glasses with ice and put them on the bar. The regulars looked over from their card games and smiled blearily.

– Hey Trish, they called over, whaddya think this is? Hollywood? And they pointed at the ripped seats and peeling decor and laughed chestily.

Trisha stuck her tongue out at them and poured the cocktails over ice.

– Here, she said, try this.

I took a cautious sip. The alcohol made me splutter.

– No, no, like this, she said, and downed hers in one. – You've got to drink them fast.

I took a bigger gulp but it made me retch.

– Ach, she said softly. – Put some orange juice in it. She leant over and poured a bottle of juice into my glass. – Have to practise if you're going to work here.

She spent the afternoon making cocktails and reading her horror novel. Whenever she got to a gruesome bit she'd call me over and read it out. It was always something really sick, like rats eating out intestines or people getting disembowelled. Every now and then she'd shake another cocktail, Screaming Orgasms, Blue Hawaiis, Zombies. – A classic, she said, as she poured the pinkish liquid into a glass.

By the end of my shift I had a row of coloured glasses slowly going flat and sticky at the end of the bar. When she went to the toilet I threw them down the sink. There was a fly trapped in my Screaming Orgasm, slowly drowning in the milky liquid, its tiny legs flailing against the sides of the glass. When I threw the drink away, it skidded down the side of the sink and lay trapped in the plughole, its wings twitching.

When Dean arrived for the evening shift, her eyes were sparkling. – Come and join me, honey, she said, twanging her vowels. – Dean, give the girl whatever she wants. She patted the barstool next to her. – Don't be shy.

Sitting close to her, I could see where her skin was beginning to pucker.

She went on about America. – Took me six months, she said, and it was only meant to take six weeks. I got lost in Las Vegas. She giggled. – Or perhaps I should say, I got held up in Las Vegas. You ever seen a gun, Mandy?

I shook my head.

– Everyone has 'em out there. I took lessons. She made her fingers into a gun barrel and pretended to aim it at me. – I loved it. She made a shooting noise. – There, gotcha, square in the chest with a forty-four.

– Arghhh. I pretended to die.

– Hehe. You're all right you are, she said, smiling, as she blew imaginary smoke from the tips of her nails.

By closing time I was warm and woozy and my head was full with the echo of Trisha's voice.

– You're a good girl. She leant over a planted a quick kiss on my cheek. – You wanna go for a drive?

Up close, I could smell the drink on her breath, warm and sweet.

– I didn't know you had a car, I said, thinking that she was much too pissed to drive.

– I don't, she said, raising her eyebrows. – It's Billy's.

When all the customers had been thrown out, grumbling their way back to their bedsits and flats to wait until we'd let them in again, we locked up and walked down the hill towards the blocks of maisonettes and the lock-up garages.

In the darkness everything seemed murky, greasy, and I felt hairs prickle under my collar. A dog barked loudly and I pressed into Trisha. She slipped her hand into the crook of my elbow and squeezed my arm.

– Mandy?

– Uh-huh? I glanced up at her. She was watching me from the corner of her eye.

– Can you keep a secret?

– I guess, I said.

– It's not mine, she said, the car.

– I thought it was your Billy's?

– Not really. Look, Mandy, it's bent. Billy's been looking after it for some friends. She pursed her lips. – So if anyone asks, you never saw it. You don't know nothing. You know customers and that, you never know who they might be talking to.

– Oh. I was quiet because I didn't know what to say, but I think she thought I disapproved.

– I mean, everyone does it round here, bit of this, bit of that, y'know. She shrugged. – Gotta keep cashflow ticking over, and it's not like that place keeps the money rolling in.

She put the key in the padlock, staggering slightly as she tried to stand still.

– Damn, she said, dropping the keys. – You do it.

The key turned sweetly in the lock, and together we lifted the door up and pushed it back, revealing the gleaming headlamps of a slick, dark Jaguar. It was an old one, I could tell from the curvy shape of the bonnet which seemed to stretch for ever.

– It's a beauty, Trisha said, patting it. – Don't make cars like this any more.

The gap between the wall and the car was narrow and I scraped the door against the concrete as I got in.

– Fucking watch it, she said sharply, raising her arm as if to cuff me.

– Sorry, I said, instinctively ducking my head.

It was like a palace. The seats were wider than sofas, all soft with plush red leather upholstery. The dashboard was polished walnut, and all the switches and handles were a shiny, glistening chrome.

– Wow, I said, before I could stop myself.

Trisha grinned and turned the key in the ignition. Everything lit up like Christmas, and dance music came pumping through the speakers too loud, making us jump.

– He got it kitted out with a stereo last week, Trisha said, holding the steering wheel. – Brrum, brrum. Where shall we go? Let's run away somewhere, you 'n' me.

When we were kids, me and Sharleen from number 53 used to pretend we were going to Blackpool. Someone dumped a Cortina at the bottom of our block. It got robbed for scraps until there was nothing left, and it was all rusty and fucked. Someone made some seats out of planks of wood and the big kids would sit in it and smoke fags and drink cans of cider. Sometimes after school we got to sit in it and pretend we were on our way to Blackpool to go on the rollercoasters. Sharleen's big brother had gone with school and, high up above the pleasure beach, with the whole of Blackpool and the seaside stretched out in front of him, he spewed. It went all over his teachers in the car in front, she said. I laughed about that so hard I wet myself. Sharleen saw it dripping all down the plank, glistening as it soaked into the wood. She looked at me and went bright red and I saw that she'd done the same thing, the rubbish crackling as the piss dripped on to the bottom of the car.

– Let's go to the beach, I said. – I want to see the sea. Let's go to Blackpool.

I don't think Trisha heard me. She was staring straight ahead, not blinking.

– We can't, she said, shaking her head. – We can't. She turned to me and her eyes were wet with creeping tears. – I hate this place you know. I hate it. She snapped off the ignition. – Pet, you don't want to listen to me moaning on. C'mon, get out. Let's go.

– But I thought . . .

– Honey, she said, bringing her face close to mine so I could smell the drink, I'm drunk as a skunk. You shouldn't've let me out of the pub.

We walked back in silence. Trisha moodily flicked a bit of gravel along the road. When we got to the pub she turned and smiled tightly, her eyes focusing over my shoulder.

– See you then, she said, turning to put her key in the door.

That night I couldn't sleep. I lay in bed, my pulse racing, thinking of us in that car, pumping like adrenalin, pushing forwards, always forwards, smooth and sexy, like a video on MTV.

When I went to work the next day Trisha wasn't there and Billy was back with a hangover. I was disappointed. I'd been looking forward to seeing her, planning conversations with her in my head.

– Remember to smile at the customers, Billy said, grimacing so I could see his fillings. – Doesn't cost anything.

He ran his hands nervously through his thinning hair, his fat gold rings catching the light. I couldn't understand what Trisha saw in him. His nose was broken into a crooked shape which made me feel sick if I looked at it too long, and when he was uptight he bounced on the balls of his feet like a boxer. He spent the rest of that day playing darts and drinking Guinness with the regulars. The fading afternoon light streamed through the frosted glass, swirls of dust moving lazily in its rays. I thought maybe she'd come down then and start telling me stories, her voice thick and dark, wrapping around my ears like smoke.

*

When I finished my shift Billy looked sorry for me. – Have a drink, bab, before you go. He patted me on the back. – It's never that bad.

One of the regulars rolled up to the bar. A big man, in a rank green overcoat, who everyone called Tic. He smiled at me, his eyes swimming behind his thick lenses.

– Orright love, he said, leaning against the bar. – Wha's a girl like yous doin'na place lie this?

– Hi Tic.

He smelled of old tobacco and pee.

– Got gorgeous legs you 'ave, gorgeous. He lunged for me with his swollen, blotchy hands.

– Leave it out, Tic, I said, moving away from him so that he stumbled slightly.

He pushed his glasses up his nose and looked confused. – Orright, orright, only joking. Pint of bitter please, Dean.

Dean looked at me and raised his eyebrows. – Right, he said. He put a pint of bitter in front of Tic.

– Ah, c'mon man, Tic said, pointing at the glass. – Gi'us more'n'at. Less fro' man, lesh fro'. I know you lot, tek a man's beer from 'um. His speech was burred and thick as if his mouth was full of treacle.

Dean squizzed a jet of beer into Tic's glass, slopping froth down the side. – That's a quid, Tic.

Tic fumbled in his coat pocket, his fat fingers trying to come together in a clumsy grasp. He finally produced a penny.

– Ah man, gi'us it on tic. Tic for Tic. He laughed so hard his chest sounded like a percolator. – Billy, he shouted, slamming his fist on the bar. – Billy, c'mere. He was going to get thrown out now for sure. – Billy man, g'us tic, tic for Tic. Tic Tack.

Billy was deliberately taking his time to finish off his game of darts. He sauntered over, raising his eyebrows at Dean.

– All right there, Tic, he said, putting his hand on Tic's shoulder and puffing out his chest so he suddenly seemed taller. – I think you've had enough now.

Tic spun round, confused. He shouted something at Billy, spitting all over him. Drunk and off-kilter, he staggered and fell forwards. Billy caught him and pushed him upright. For a moment Billy's face crunched in anger, and I thought he was going to punch Tic.

– C'mon now, c'mon now, he said. – Time to go home.

Tic stopped resisting and went quiet, as if suddenly aware that he was making a scene. He let Billy lead him to the door and stumbled over the mat as he left. Billy came back to the bar and tapped on it with his keyring, bouncing a little on his feet. He was staring at Tic's pint slowly going flat on the drip tray.

– Bin it, he said, tapping the glass.

She came in a few minutes later with a load of other women, all done up. I didn't recognize her at first; waiting to see her all day I had almost forgotten what she looked like. They were all giggling, doubling over their shopping bags.

– Hiya kid, she said when she saw me. – You still here?

I smiled at her as she dumped her bags behind the bar. She turned towards me and winked before rejoining the screeching throng of women, who were all making a big display of sitting down, wobbling and laughing and spilling their shopping.

I picked up my fags and pulled up the hood of my coat.

– See you then, I said.

No one turned round.

When I got home the flat was cold and dark. The meter had run out of electricity and it was too late to buy any more. I made tea with cold water and stuffed down a stale slice of bread. I poured myself a Bacardi from a bottle I'd robbed from the pub, coughing as it burnt the back of my throat. I didn't really like the taste of it unless it was in Coke, but at least it was warming. I sat in the dark for hours, watching the city panning out for miles, lights twinkling and blurring through the distance. The whole city seemed jewelled with possibility, unrolling like an adventure beneath me.

I wanted a car then more than anything. I wanted to disappear down every street and road and cul-de-sac until I knew what was there, until I could map the whole maze of streets on to the back of my hand.

I went to work in my best top and jeans. I even did my hair proper, teasing my fringe into neat spikes at the front.

She was sitting at the end of the bar flicking through the *Sun*. I started collecting glasses, rattling them deliberately as I put them in the washer. She looked up and smiled.

– You look smart, she said. – Off somewhere special?

I shrugged, finding that I couldn't remember any of the things I wanted to say.

– We're off at the weekend, she said, hunching her shoulders up like a kid. – Me 'n' Billy, we're off to Blackpool.

– You going in the car? I asked. – I thought that was our idea.

She frowned at me. – Sshh. You'll get us in trouble.

After that the draymen showed up with a delivery and she busied off to deal with it. I could hear her down in the cellar with the men. The rolling barrels scraped on the concrete and reverberated through the floor.

– What's up with you? she said, as she brushed past me to pour herself a double brandy afterwards. – Got a face like a wet weekend. You were a happy puppy when you came in this morning. Now look at you. She pinched my cheek and winked. – You don't make the best of yourself, you know. You'd look good with some lipstick on. Here, she said, giggling, let me touch you up. She winked and got a lipstick out of her pocket. – Pucker up.

She smeared a greasy line of Burnished Bronze across my lips, her face uncomfortably close. When she was done I looked at her and snarled like I'd seen the models do in magazines.

– That's better, she said. – Have a look. She pointed at the mirror behind the optics.

I thought I looked garish and my lips felt muffled. They tingled underneath the slick of make-up. We smiled at each other in the mirror.

– See, you're a pretty girl. She put her arm lightly across my shoulders.

I froze, hardly daring to breathe, a hot blush creeping up my cheeks.

– Bloody lesbians.

I jumped. It was Billy, stood at the end of the bar, watching us. I wondered how long he'd been there.

– Taken you under her wing has she? She's good at that.

– Just having a laugh, Billy, Trisha said. – No harm in that.

Billy tapped his keyring on the bar. – Give it a rest, Trisha, he said. – She's only a kid.

She hardly spoke to me after that. She fussed about the place, doing things that she never did, rearranging the optics and going out for a basket of dried flowers to put in the Ladies.

– Gotta keep it looking tidy, eh Mandy? Give the bar a wipe down, sweetheart. While there's no one in.

She even hoovered the back stairs.

By the time I finished my shift she was sat back at the bar, flicking through the papers.

– Eh, Mandy, she said. – C'mere. She caught my eye, holding my gaze long enough to make me look away. – Sweetheart.

I stood next to her. She snaked an arm round my waist, pulling me up close.

– Meet me tonight. By the garages. Half eleven. She tweaked a spike of my hair. – Get us a vodka and orange before you go, there's a good girl.

Time couldn't pass quick enough. I necked a few Bacardis, thinking they would calm me down, but they made me light-headed and nauseous. I had a bath and washed my hair again, spent time scrubbing the smell of the pub out of my skin. I rubbed myself over with stuff from the Body Shop, my hands shaking so much I spilled loads on the carpet. I spent ages in front of the bathroom mirror. From certain angles I could make myself look perky, cheeky, cute; from others I seemed monstrous, abnormal, neither girl nor boy.

She didn't show up till half twelve.

– Thought you'd've gone home by now.

– Nearly did, I said, shivering. – It's bloody freezing out here.

She laughed. – Won't do you any harm, young thing like you. She grabbed my hand. – C'mon then, let's hit the road.

We dropped off the kerb with a slick dip of suspension.

– This thing's so smooth, Trisha said, before crunching the gears. – For an old car.

For a few miles she drove slowly, tutting at herself every time she messed up a gear change. We got to a box junction and she changed up instead of down. The car started to kangaroo across the road.

– I thought you said you could drive, I said, gripping the seat belt as she tried to get the car to stop.

– I can, she said, just never passed me test. Don't worry, honey. I did loads of driving in America.

She started the car again, taking her time to accelerate. By the time we got to the ring road we'd done a few junctions without stalling or crunching and Trisha had settled more comfortably into the seat. She even turned the stereo up so that the boom of the bass made the chassis rattle against the frame of the car.

– These old things weren't meant for modern music, Trisha said, turning the volume up even higher.

We whipped into the city, the car light on the road. In the underpass Trisha put her foot down, the mosaic patterns blurring into a fuzz of colour. We flew past throngs of clubbers and the trundling taxis that were taking them home. Everywhere there were people, moving and shouting, huddling in pools of lamplight. We slid through the centre in a trance, past the Town Hall, dipping down through another tunnel, turning sharply off a six-way roundabout and out on to the Expressway.

– It's like America this is, Trisha said, as she swerved between lanes. – Got roads like this in LA.

The signs above us read Coventry, London, Manchester.

– Where d'you wanna go? she said.

– You choose.

– Tell you what, I'll close my eyes and then whatever lane we end up in, that's where we'll go.

– No! I mean, don't close your eyes. Please.

She laughed, sharply turning the wheel to change lanes. – Too late. A lorry sounded its horn loudly behind us. – We're going to London.

We passed out of the centre up the dual carriageway, speeding through suburbs, high streets, industrial estates, warehouses, towerblocks, small pockets of houses and shops, on and on for miles. Just as it seemed that the whole world was made of concrete, the buildings began to thin out and give way to scrubby fields.

Coming off the junction to the motorway she undercut a Transit to move into the fast lane. I pressed my legs to the floor, my feet rigid against the slipmat, and looked at the speedometer. We were doing eighty-five.

– This is more like it, eh? she said, not taking her eyes off the road.

– Yeh, I said, not wanting conversation. All it would take was one flick of the wrist and we'd be wasted against the crash barrier. I wondered whether Mum would cry. I could see her standing by the grave, clutching the Bastard's arm, wiping away her tears with his hankie.

– Yeeha, Trisha screamed over the urgent pumping of the music. – All *right*.

My teeth hurt from clenching my jaw. Trisha was grinning and giggling manically.

– Isn't this fun? she said. – You gotta learn to drive, it's excellent. I'll teach you. She took a hand from the steering wheel and dropped it casually on my lap. – You're a pretty girl you are, Mandy.

– Mmm, I said, not daring to take my eyes off the road. The hand in my lap was spreading its fingers, moving them in insistent circles around the inside of my thigh. I felt my heart start pumping in time with the music.

– *Let the music lift you up, whoo yeah,* Trisha sang, *higher and higher.*

Suddenly we were doing a hundred, a hundred and ten. Trisha put her foot to the floor and the car started whining underneath us. For a second I thought we were going to take off. I wriggled in my seat, not knowing whether to notice the hand that was circling between my legs, making me feel hot and dizzy. I couldn't bear it, but I didn't want her to stop. My stomach fizzed with acid.

– I wanna get out, I said, suddenly overwhelmed. – I'm gonna be sick.

– For fuck's sake. Trisha took her eyes off the road to look at me. – Wind down your window.

The air howled in. Trisha squeezed the fleshy part of my thigh. She was going too fast.

– Stop it, I said. – STOP. Please Trisha, stop it.

She took her hand back and looked ahead grimly, putting her foot on the accelerator. The car was squealing and the speedo was nudging a hundred and twenty.

– Chicken.

I didn't want it to be like this. I sat up straighter. – I'll be all right, I said, trying to breathe deeply.

It crashed over me in a wave, and before I could register what was happening, I'd thrown up over my shoes.

– Oh Jesus girl, not all over the car, Trisha said, slowing the car with a jerk.

I retched again, this time sending a spray of vomit across the walnut dashboard. Trisha flinched like she'd been scalded.

– For God's sake keep it in, Mandy.

We cut across from the outside lane and screeched to a halt on the hard shoulder. Trisha reached across me to open the car door.

– Get out! Get out! She undid my seat belt and pushed me out of the car. – Oh Christ, it's everywhere.

I crouched on the tarmac by the car, my stomach heaving like a stuck record. Finally, weak and giddy, I stood up, leaning against the solidity of the car for support.

– Geddoffit! Trisha shrieked. – I don't want you throwing up on it again. Jesus it stinks in here. She was frantically swabbing the dashboard with a tissue. – He's gonna know I've been pissing about with the car, you silly little cow. Why didn't you tell me you got carsick?

I giggled nervously, which seemed to make her even more cross.

– I *knew* this was a bad idea. She banged the car door shut and shouted at me through the window. – You can bloody well find your own way home. Silly little slag.

She slammed her foot down and the car bucked forwards on to the motorway. Within seconds her tail lights had slipped out of view.

I turned to face the traffic. Squinting against the blaze of oncoming headlights and struggling to steady my breathing, I stuck out my thumb.

Biographical Notes

Julia Bell was born in Wales in 1971. She came to Birmingham to study at the university and later became a member of Tindal Street Fiction Group. In 1996 she graduated with an MA in Creative Writing from the University of East Anglia, where she now teaches Creative Writing, Literature and Publishing. She is the co-editor of the forthcoming *Creative Writing Coursebook* (Macmillan, 2000) and the literary journal, *Pretext* (UEA, 1999).

Steve Bishop was born in Liverpool. He moved to Birmingham to study at the university and has lived in Moseley ever since. He is currently working on his first novel, *Foxy Lady*. This is his first published short story.

Gemma Blackshaw was born in Essex, and studied English and Art History at Birmingham University. She is currently working on her Master's degree and completing a collection of short stories.

Gul Davis was born in 1973. His experience as a sufferer of dyslexia, the dysfunction and breakdown of his family, of mental illness and periods in psychiatric institutions, shadow, shape and define the colour of his writing.

Jackie Gay was born in Birmingham and travelled in Europe, Asia, the Far East and Africa before returning home to write. She is a member of Tindal Street Fiction Group and has had stories published in *Raw Edge*, *Quality Women's Fiction* and *London Magazine*.

Neil Hall was born in Nottingham and grew up in a small village in Derbyshire. He is due to start a Broadcast Journalism post-graduate diploma this year. He has had poems published in local arts board magazines but this is his first published story.

Charlie Hill is 28 years old. He has lived in Birmingham all his life and drinks and plays pool in Balsall Heath.

Ranjit Khutan is 26 and lives in Walsall with his partner. After graduating from Essex University with a Russian Studies degree he returned to Birmingham to work in health promotion projects. 'B22' is an adaptation of his play which won a prize in the Young Writers' programme at the Royal Court Theatre and received a five-week performance in London.
Sarah Martin grew up in Southwell, Nottinghamshire. She is currently studying for a BA in English and hopes to take up a career in broadcasting.
Andrew Newsham was born in Burnley in 1975. Having travelled the world he now lives in Moseley and writes and performs comedy.
Mark Newton was born in Lincoln in 1977. He moved to Birmingham in 1995 to attend university and has recently finished studying. He intends to travel to Japan to teach English.
Nick Rendall was born in London but grew up a Brummie. This story was written for an English exam when he was 15. He promotes drum 'n' bass nights in Birmingham.
David Savill is 23 going on 50 and has lived in Stourbridge, Hagley, Moseley, Budapest and Tuzla. He has been writing prose since he wrote off everything else at school.
Edward Scrivens is 17, and took up writing to avoid doing serious work. This is his first published story.
Rob Smith was born in Birmingham and educated at Queensbridge and Highgate Schools, Birmingham, and King's College, London, where he studied English, and in many other informal places before, between and since. He spent two years teaching in Sudan and lives in Birmingham with his family.
Alison Waller was born and brought up in Bedford. She has recently graduated from the University of Birmingham with a degree in English, and would like to become an expert on narrative studies. First she plans to travel in Europe and Africa to get life experience and ideas for her writing.